I0847430

Sweet Addictions

J.S. Mercier

Copyright © 2024 by JS Mercier

All rights reserved. No part of this book may be reproduced, scanned, or distributed in any form in any means without the express, written permission of the author, except in the case of brief quotations in book reviews. The unauthorized reproduction or distribution of this work is illegal.

To request permissions, email the author at jsmercierauthor@gmail.com.

This is a work of fiction. Names, characters, places, and incidents are the product of the author's imagination and any resemblance to any organization, event, or person, living or dead, is purely coincidental or being used fictitiously.

Content Warning

Sweet Addictions is a dark, high-heat retelling of Little Red Riding Hood. It features explicit and sometimes disturbing content, including voyeurism, a cancer diagnosis, discussions of drug overdose, stalking, murder, and torture. Check your triggers before reading.

Listen Along

Interested in listening to the songs that are featured in and helped inspire the story? Check out the Spotify playlist for this story, and all my others!

Contents

Prologue

My world narrows down to the movement of the doctor's mouth. His words are drowned out by the growing sound of static in my ears, making it impossible for me to understand what he's saying. His words mean absolutely nothing to me.

After the word "cancer," what other words could matter?

Gran's tightening grip brings me back to myself, snapping me out of my stupor.

"I'm sorry, I lost you for a second," I admit, giving both Gran and the doctor a strained smile before straightening in my seat and squeezing Gran's hand back. "So, what is the treatment plan? I'll be coming home from school so she has help doing whatever she needs."

"Over my dead body!" Gran snarls, smacking my arm and glaring at me as if her comment wasn't hitting too close to home directly after receiving that diagnosis. "You're not leaving school! I'll be fine, Penelope."

I turn to her, eyes narrowed in a challenge.

"Watch me."

Chapter One

"I can't believe they fired you, Gran! We should sue them or something." I huff before taking a sip of my soda. "That's discrimination! It's discrimination, right? It has to be. What do they expect you to do?"

"They didn't fire me, Penny," she insists, exasperated. "I can't do the job they hired me for while I'm in chemo. I'm not physically capable, you know that. I went to talk to Rob and instead of letting me quit, he gave me a year's severance and insurance so I don't have to worry about anything while in treatment. He said I'd been with them so long I was like family. Hell, I practically helped raise that boy. If I recover and gain my strength back he said a job will be waiting for me."

"Well... good."

That took the wind out of my sails faster than anything else could, and she knows me well enough to realize what happened because she laughs and takes a bite of bread. "We'll be fine, you'll see. I have insurance and a paycheck for a year. That's more than enough time for treatment, and once I'm cancer-free I'll be able to work again." She narrows her eyes and points at me with an aggressively bossy finger, "Just in time for you to be able to start back to school next fall."

I love that Gran has a positive outlook on this situation, but I'm more of a realist. She may have health insurance, but it's not the best. Based on my research, one round of chemo can cost tens of thousands out of pocket. We don't have that kind of money. I barely saved up enough money for two years' tuition working part time while in high school and three years of full time after I graduated. Now, whether she wants to or not, we'll be using what I have left to cover her expenses. Even using my life savings, though, I'll have to find a job so we can stay afloat.

"Gran, school may have to wait."

"Over my dead body!"

"Stop saying that!" I bark without meaning to. "We need the money for your treatment and to live in general, Gran. I have to get a job as it is."

"Absolutely not, Penelope Grace Channing!" she snaps, opening her mouth to scold me further when she's cut off by a vaguely familiar voice.

"Penny?"

Our attention snaps to the side of our table at the same time, my frustration rising as I hear someone other than my Grandma call me by my nickname. Our visitor looks incredibly familiar, but his name is eluding me. Tall and broad, he's handsome in a boyish way. I examine the cleanly shaved jawline and his one dimple finally jogs my memory.

"Trevor?"

His smile turns blinding when I recognize him, and he nods happily. "Yeah! How are you? Man, it's been so long! You look great!"

"Oh, thanks," I respond, standing to give him a brief hug since it's obvious he wants one. "Gran, this is Trevor, we went to high school together. Trevor, this is my Gran, Tabitha Channing."

"It's so nice to finally meet you, Ms. Channing. Penny always spoke so highly of you."

"Oh stop that, it's just Tabitha. Why don't you join us?" I hit Gran with a glower that makes it obvious she's overstepped, but she simply smiles, winks as if she thinks she's doing me a favor, and pulls a chair from the table next to us so Trevor can join. "We haven't ordered yet."

"Oh, I couldn't possibly intrude," he insists, obviously full of crap because he takes his seat and scoots up to the table while he declines.

Lovely.

We chat for a while, catching up until Gran drops the cancer bomb on Trevor, then excuses herself to run to the bathroom like a scheming coward. She loves doing that. Hitting someone with some crazy information and running so she can't answer any follow-up questions.

"Shit, Penny. I'm so sorry," Trevor tells me when she's a few tables away. "That's got to be rough."

"It is, but the doctors said she has a good prognosis. We'll get her through treatment and she'll be fine."

"About that," he hesitates, "I wasn't trying to pry but I happened to hear you as I was walking up to say hello. Do you have any leads on jobs? It sounded like you need one."

I start to feel embarrassed but remind myself that's stupid. Everyone needs to work! "I do, preferably night shift work so I can take Gran to her appointments. Why? Got one you want to give me?" I joke, poking him lightly on his arm. I pause, feeling my eyes popping wide as he waffles his head from side to side.

"Well..." he sighs, wincing. "Look, please don't take this the wrong way."

"Ok..."

"Remember my uncle? Felix?"

"I think so. The one who wears a lot of gold jewelry, right?" I ask, wincing at the memory.

"That's him," he chuckles. "He has a few businesses, and I've been managing one of them for the past year. We're always looking to hire." He pauses and takes a deep breath. "Short version? Yes. I have one for you if you want it."

That sounds ominous.

"What's the long version?"

"Well, I have a few different positions I could offer you. They each have different earning potential."

"It's legal, right?" I don't care what I have to do to make sure Gran is taken care of, but I'd prefer for it to be legal.

"Of course!" he answers, hands thrown up in a placating gesture. "Everything is one hundred percent legal. It's a club, so we have positions for waitresses and bartenders with flexible schedules. You can work as much or as little as you want."

"What else is there?"

"Huh?"

"You said a few. Bartending and waitressing aren't offensive job offerings. I'm still waiting on the punchline."

Trevor chuckles and takes a sip of his sweet tea. "I forgot how smart you are. It's a gentleman's club. I don't know if you'd have any interest in stripping, but it's a high-end club and our dancers can make up to a few thousand per night."

I feel awful when I spray my drink on his hand. "Thou–" I cough, clearing my throat as I snatch up a napkin to wipe his hand. "Did you say a few *thousand* per night?"

"I did. Because of that, though, we're very picky when it comes to who we hire. I can guarantee you a job as a waitress or bartender, but not a dancer. You'll have to audition if it's something you're interested in."

Gran catches my attention as she exits the restroom across the restaurant. I don't want her to know I'm stripping if I end up doing that. She did it when she was younger and always said she wanted better for me, which I never understood. She loved doing it! If it made her happy, it shouldn't matter what it was. Plus, that shit is *hard*.

"I am," I answer quietly, "but I'd rather Gran not know. I'll tell her you have a waitressing job available." At his nod, I relax my shoulders and smile at Gran.

"Trevor has an opening at the club he manages and said it's mine if I want it." It's not even a lie since that's also an option. "It'll be night work, so I'll be able to take you to all of your appointments."

"Penny, I don't–"

"Gran, please. I've worked since I was fourteen. I don't feel right without a job, and I want to be able to be with you for my own sake, in addition to yours. This is the best possible scenario."

Chapter Two

I spent the last two days preparing for my audition. Part of me feels like I should have told Trevor I have some experience, but the larger part wants to see his reaction when he figures it out. I've technically never stripped before, but I have almost two years of training in pole work. One of my closest friends from nursing school was stripping to pay her way, and we made a deal. I'd babysit her kids on the nights both she and her husband had to work, and in return, she taught me how to pole dance. I still think I got the best side of that deal since I could study in peace after the kids went to sleep, and I didn't have to pay for a gym membership because training with her was more than enough of a workout.

I dropped Gran off at home after lunch with Trevor and called Halla for a much-needed pep talk. She not only gave me the boost of confidence I needed, but she also helped me choose my best routine, encouraged me to wear the cape and shoes she gave me for my Halloween costume last year, and found me a last-minute practice space. We even FaceTimed so I could pick out the perfect outfit. Having her in my corner, even if she isn't here physically, made all the difference. I'll simply pretend it's any other session with her and forget anyone else is around since, according to her, the lights should help with the illusion that I'm alone.

Trevor asked me to show up after hours so I wouldn't have to dance in front of the entire staff. I told him it was fine, if I got the job I'd have to dance in front of far more people than the staff, but he insisted it was normal protocol for auditions. That means showing up at a strip club at 4:00 a.m.

The flashing red neon over the main entrance of The Den fills me both with amusement and a bit of trepidation. While the costume I chose for my audition couldn't have been more ironic if I'd planned it, the blood red, buzzing sign also fills me with a sense of nervousness. A large man is standing in front of the door and he scrutinizes me heavily as I approach.

"Hi," I say, trying to force as much confidence into my tone as possible. "I'm here to see Trevor?" Awesome! Nothing like completely canceling out any confidence he may think I have by asking a question instead of making a statement.

"Penny?" the man asks, his voice deep and unaffected. My spine stiffens and I forget my nerves as I hit him with a glare.

"Penelope," I growl through clenched teeth. I hate nicknames, I always have. Gran is the only person I've ever allowed to give me one, and that's because she's called me Penny pretty much since birth. Trevor hasn't earned that, and this mountain of douche sure hasn't.

His eyebrows shoot up as if he's amused, but he only nods and tilts his head to the door as he moves to open it for me. "Changing rooms are in the back to the left. Check-in with Mina, she should still be back there and will get you taken care of. Trevor will be ready when you are."

"Thanks," I tell him, smiling an apology. It's not his fault Trevor didn't give him my real name, so he had no way of knowing. I'm definitely going to make sure he doesn't use it again though. The inside of the club is an odd mix of luxurious and dingy, probably because the lights being on reveal issues that the open-hour darkness of the club can easily hide. Trevor is standing by the bar on the opposite side of the room next to his uncle, and they're shaking hands with a man who is surrounded by a wall of muscle that looks so similar to the mountain outside it makes me wonder if the doorman works for the club, or him.

My entrance catches Trevor's attention and he nods to me stiffly and points to the door I was already heading to. His distraction catches the attention of everyone with him and they all turn to follow my movement through the club. His uncle looks as sleezy as ever, but it's the man they're talking to that makes my step stutter.

He's gorgeous.

I have never seen such brilliant blue eyes before, and for a heartbeat, I fall into them. His slow blink jolts me out of my stupor, causing me to blush and quickly look away. I hurry to the back room to find Mina, but luckily don't have to search long because as soon as I'm three steps into what appears to be a mixture between a locker room and the backstage at a theater company a woman in her thirties pops her head out of an office door and smiles.

"Hey Sugar!" she chirps. "You must be Penny!"

I am going to strangle Trevor!

"Hi. It's Penelope, actually."

She tilts her head to the side and examines me for a moment, then nods like the man from the front door. "That does suit you better. I'm Mina, come on back! We have an empty vanity over here and you can either change here or in that back area," she rattles off, pointing to a curtained-off section of the room. "If you can write your song info on here and note any lighting requests I can take this to the DJ so he can queue it up for you. Is there anything else you need?"

"Thank you," I sigh, putting my heavy bag down next to the chair. "And no. Oh! Wait, I was told I was only going to be auditioning for Trevor. He said no one should be here except him and the DJ but it looks like there are a lot of other men, too. Am I auditioning for them as well?"

"Oh, no! They're here for a meeting and should be leaving any minute. I'm actually surprised they're still here."

"OK, thanks. I should be ready in about ten minutes," I smile as I hand her back a sticky note with my song choice and a few lighting notes written down.

"Perfect! I'll take this to the DJ now and head back into my office," she says, pointing back to the room she initially popped her head out of. "When you're ready, just holler and we'll get you started!"

She sashays off in a stride that is part sex and part limp, and I try to force her out of my mind so I can focus on getting ready. I've danced like this before in front of Halla and a few of her friends, but never an actual audience, and it's been over five years since my last ballet recital. Knowing the men that were out there won't be hanging around for my first attempt at a performance makes me feel better, and oddly, so does Mina being here. Maybe I'll ask her to watch so I know there's a woman in my corner.

I get ready quickly, knowing the longer I dawdle the more nervous I'll be. Popping into the curtained-off area I slip on my new white lace corset and panty set with garter and stockings I purchased under a wrap version of a black French maid dress without the apron. Returning to the vanity I take a seat and fluff my curled hair, making sure I don't need to fix anything, then use ribbon to create pigtails that hang down my chest. My makeup is already on and heavier than usual, years of ballet proving how washed out the lights can make me look, so after a touch-up of my bronzer and a fresh coat of crimson lipstick I pull on the ridiculously high heels.

Standing, I grab my cloak and secure it as I move over to the wall mirror. I don't even look like myself! I've always liked my subtle, natural beauty, but seeing myself like this? It fills me with a confidence I don't think I've ever had before. Mina's whistle startles me and I spin to meet her gaze.

"Damn, Sugar! You're like a whole new person, aren't you? Are you ready?"

I smile, realizing I like her. Maybe we could be friends if I get the job.

"Ready."

Mina directs me to the edge of the stage and kisses my cheek for luck before scuttling off to the DJ booth to tell him I'm ready to go. They've turned the house lights off completely, and when the stage lights go down I lift my hood so it covers the top of my face and take my mark. Red lights brighten and the reverberation that signals the beginning of "Physical (You're SO)" by Nine Inch Nails begins thrumming through my body. I move with a sensual grace from the back of the stage to the pole, stepping in front so I can lean against it. With one hand above my head gripping the pole and one below, I slide down and tilt my head back so my hood falls away, revealing my face. My hips begin to sway with the music and I straighten to hook my leg around the pole and begin to spin.

I've almost lost myself in the music like I used to, but Trent's voice pulls me back and reminds me it's time to remove my cloak. I unlatch the clasp at my neck and let one side drop, twirling the fabric a bit with one hand at the same time he wants to twist and shout. I toss it off to the side so I can run my hands along my body, accentuating my curves until the chorus begins and I grab an end of each ribbon tying my hair back and release my locks. Dropping the pieces of fabric to the floor I shake my hair out in a way that hopefully causes it to look like I've been ravished, then move back to the pole. When I've climbed halfway up the pole I lock my legs around it and bend backwards so I can untie my dress. I arch my back and roll my midsection so when my arms drop back the fabric falls free, dropping to the ground and revealing my lingerie.

The red gel lighting has made my already crimson hair even more vibrant, and the white of my remaining clothing is tinted as well, making me practically glow. I run my hands over my body again, now hanging upside down, and roll my hips into my hand when I slip my fingers between my legs. Blue eyes pop into my mind, and the jolt of pleasure they send through me causes my fingers to linger a bit longer than I planned in an attempt to ease a bit of the pressure that's begun building.

Releasing some of the tension in my legs I allow myself to slide slowly to the ground, stretching my arms out above my head and bowing my back so my breasts are raised high for a moment. I roll over abruptly, swinging my hair in a wide arc so it ends up draping in front of my face as I prowl on hands and knees down the length of the stage. My senses are so focused inward that when I finally reach the end and look up I'm shocked into immobility for a few beats.

Blue eyes.

Vibrant, shining blue eyes, filled with a hunger I've never experienced before.

Afraid I'll be stuck if I continue meeting his gaze I spin in place and crawl my way back to the pole. If my legs are spread a little wider and my hips are rolling a little more aggressively than normal, it's purely a coincidence.

Pinky promise.

When I reach the pole I grab onto it and pull myself up until I can move into the splits parallel to it. The song is at the fever pitch at this point, so I use the rest of the time to showcase my strongest skills. By the end of the song, I'm breathing hard and thinking of nothing but the man who is watching me. The lights dim while one hand is back between my legs and the other is gripping my hair, and there's a moment of complete silence before Mina and a few others begin cheering and clapping.

The house lights come up abruptly, pulling me out of my trance. Breath heaving I turn, unable to stop myself from seeking out the man who has been captivating my thoughts since I first saw him. I expect to meet his eyes once more, but all I find is his back as he walks away from me.

JAGER

The moment my eyes lock on the young woman who just entered the club a wave of possession rolls through me so strongly I don't think I've ever felt anything like it. She's petite, with milky skin and hair so brilliantly red it's a color I've only ever seen come out of a salon. Somehow, though, it looks natural on her. As soon as the door to the backstage area closes behind her, I return my attention to Felix and his nephew.

"Who is she?" I ask, my affect flat as I interrupt whatever desperate bullshit Felix is throwing my way.

"Her? No one." Trevor insists, spine stiffening. "Just another girl who wants a job. They're a dime a dozen, really."

"I didn't ask you for your fucking opinion, kid. I asked who she is."

"Her name is Penny," Felix sputters, hand on the kid's chest in an attempt to keep him from saying whatever stupid thing looked to be on the tip of his tongue. "She went to school with Trevor."

"Penelope," Mike corrects as he steps up to my side. He'd been watching the door while they waited for the girl to arrive. "I called her Penny and thought she was going to scold me like my elementary school teacher." He laughs, shocking me when he smiles as if she impressed him. No one impresses Mike, except Mina. "She didn't look like it at first, but she's got spine."

"Thank you for coming by tonight, Mr. Conri. I told Penn... *Penelope,* I would be the only one watching her. I don't want to break my word."

The bartender walking by places an amber liquid filled glass on the table at the end of the stage, and I have a marvelous idea. Not only will it give me what I want, but I'll have the added pleasure of pissing off this little runt who thinks he can tell me what the fuck to do.

"I don't give a fuck about you and your word," I tell him, snapping my fingers at the bartender for my own drink and leaving them all behind as I head to the table in question. "I'm staying right here. You can do whatever you want, as long as it's not by me."

I dismiss all of them and take a seat at the center table at the end of the runway, accepting my drink and leaning back in my chair to relax until show time. Trevor is arguing with Felix, attempting to convince him to make me leave, but for once Felix is smart enough to realize the right thing to do. Obviously, the kid has no idea who I really am.

I fucking own them.

When the lights finally dim I'm expecting some new popular pop or R&B song to sound out. Instead, Nine Inch Nails plays and I'm so fucking thankful I'm sitting behind this table, because the song paired with seeing this crimson goddess on the stage in front of me makes me painfully hard. I don't give a fuck who knows I'm attracted to her, but the thick cloak makes her look almost fragile, and for the first time in my life seeing something fragile doesn't make me want to watch it break.

It makes me want to protect her.

She dances with skill, talent showing on the pole and in her floor work, and I know that this little drop of fire will take this pretentious shithole up a few notches. They like to say they're a high end gentlemen's club, but it's a dump.

With this tiny creature headlining? With my help they may just be able to stand up to that claim.

My cock hardens to the point of pain when she crawls toward me, her hair obscuring most of her face. The flashing lights reflect off her eyes, her blown pupils showing me how much she likes what she's doing. When she's finally close enough to me for the spotlight to illuminate some of my face she realizes I'm not her friend and freezes for a moment before spinning away from me.

Not before I can see her take me in and suck a plump bottom lip into her mouth, though, and the image of her sucking my cock between those pouty red lips flashes through me as I watch the rest of her routine. Her movements have become even more sensual, letting me know she's affected by me, too. The song ends with her suspended in air, back bowed with one hand between her legs and the other in her hair.

I rise before the house lights come up and adjust my dick in my pants. Mike stands from the table behind me and I jerk my head toward the stage, directing him to ensure she's paid for her dance. He nods and makes his way to Mina, which gives Felix the opportunity to intercept me before I make it to the door. The only acknowledgement I give him is two words:

"Hire her."

Chapter Three

"Oh my gosh, Sugar, that was incredible!"

My breath is still coming in heavy pants with no sign of slowing down. If this had been a normal performance I'd be calming already, but the combination of the exertion and the mysterious man? My body and mind are on fire! I've never seen anyone so handsome, and knowing he was watching me without my knowledge sends a thrill through me.

"Thank you!" I sigh, happy with what I can recall of the performance. "Do you think I'll get the job?"

"If they don't hire you I'll walk and we'll start a club on our own!" she assures me, pulling me in for a hug. "Ok, that may be a bit much, but you're amazing! You even got a tip." Her eyebrows wiggle aggressively and the ridiculousness of the gesture makes me laugh, finally helping me slow my heart rate a bit.

"Is that normal? I thought this was just an audition."

"Well, Mr. Conri isn't usually here so I can't really say for sure."

"Oh my God," I breathe, "there has to be some sort of mistake!" She's shoved a wad of hundreds into my hand, and there has to be at least twenty bills there. "I don't... where did this come from?"

"Mikey brought it. You earned it."

"Who is Mikey?" Is he the handsome man I locked eyes with at the end of the stage? He doesn't look like a Mikey. I still can't believe he stayed to watch! And where the heck was Trevor? Was he even watching? How can I get the job if he wasn't?

"Mike is my honey. I think he was at the door when you came in? I know Mr. Conri had him posted out there during his meeting."

"Why would your boyfriend give me this kind of money?" This isn't making any sense! Why isn't she angry with me?

"It's not from him, silly. It's from Mr. Conri."

"Who is that? Why do you keep mentioning him?" I'm almost positive that Conri isn't Trevor or his uncle's last name.

"He's the older guy Felix was meeting with. He ended up staying to watch your audition. I'm sure you saw him at the end of the stage?"

"I... did. I just don't—"

"Penny!" Trevor calls, pushing his way through the back door and startling me into dropping my money.

"Darn it, Trevor!" I scold. "Don't scare me like that! And *don't* call me Penny! You know my name."

"Sorry," he replies, face heating slightly as he rubs the back of his neck while looking at his feet. The cash littering the floor catches his eye and his brow furrows, but he drops down and helps me gather it together. Once again standing, I count the cash and my jaw almost drops to the floor. There's more than two thousand dollars here! "Listen, I'm not sure if this is the best fit—"

"Trevor MacIntyre!" Mina shrieks, hands on hips and something other than a smile gracing her lovely mouth for the first time since I've met her. "You'd better be making a statement about how *this club* may not be good enough for *her*, because she's phenomenal!"

"Uh... well, are you sure you want to do this?" Trevor asks, handing me the few bills he picked up for me. "Think about your Gran."

"I am thinking about my Gran, Trevor. If I can make even close to this each week, or gosh, even in a month, I'll be able to afford whatever treatment she needs!"

"You can make close to that as a waitress instead," he claims. Why doesn't he want me to strip?

"Did you not... was I not good enough?" I ask, feeling small now, when I felt so incredibly powerful only moments before he entered the room.

"No! No you're amazing! I just know you said you wanted to keep it from her. I want to make sure you're comfortable with whatever you do."

"Thank you," I sigh, clutching the cash to my chest and accepting my cloak when Mina wraps it around my shoulders. I didn't realize I'd been shivering from the cold until the thick fabric was wrapped around me. "I'm happy to do both. I don't know if that's possible, but you know I like to work."

"Some girls do it," Mina interjects. "You're not going to have anything to worry about, sugar. We'll get you on stage and you'll be one of the most popular girls right away! You'll see."

"Trevor?" He hasn't said outright that I got the job yet, so I wait to hear what he has to say.

He sighs and runs his fingers through his hair. "Yeah, alright. You've got the job. Mina will get all of your paperwork handled and put you on the schedule. Just... if you hate it there's no problem with switching to waitressing only, ok?"

"Thanks, Trevor!" I chirp, launching myself forward to wrap him in a true hug.

I always loved my workouts with Halla, but I never thought I'd be able to do it in front of anyone other than the girls that sometimes joined us. The rush I got tonight was something I hadn't ever expected, but I want to keep chasing it.

Especially if Mr. Conri is at the end of the stage.

Mina and I worked out a schedule that will help me start out slow. It'll help me get acclimated to my new environment and allow me time to create routines and get costumes that I'll need. When I arrive home from my audition, Gran is in the kitchen making her coffee. I was hoping to get home while she still slept, but luckily I thought ahead and removed the makeup and changed in the locker room before leaving.

"Morning, Gran," I sigh in a mixture of exhaustion and happiness. "Did you sleep well?"

"I did. How was your interview?" She pauses to pour cream into her mug, "I still wish you'd reconsider. You don't need to work; we'll be fine."

"Enough, Gran. We've talked about this. I need to work." I wrap my arms around her from behind and drop my chin onto her shoulder. "And I need to be there with you for your appointments too. They're both important to me."

"Well, then?"

"I got it!" I squeal, letting my happiness finally shine through. I felt so amazing on that stage, lost in the music and the man I'd glimpsed before and during my set.

"I even made some tips already! I should be making some good money there, so hopefully I won't have to work too much."

"I'm so glad. It'll be nice to have some evenings with you, you know. My shows aren't as fun without you playing along with me."

"I'll still spend some evenings at home, I promise." A yawn catches me by surprise, and I cover my mouth before she sticks her fingers in it. Her way of teaching me manners as a child was never very... mannerly.

"Go get some rest, Penny. We don't have anything going on today."

"Ok, Gran. Love you."

"Love you more!"

I trudge up the stairs and to my bedroom at the end of the hall, dropping my bag by the door to my bathroom and clumsily stripping in a much less sexy way on my way to the bed. I pull my covers back and fall face first into my pillows, snuggling under the warm comforter and falling asleep to the vision of beautiful, blue eyes.

Chapter Four

It's been months since my audition, and although I've always watched out for him I haven't seen Mr. Conri since that night. He haunts my dreams, but that's all I've been able to have of him.

Dreams.

Speaking of my dreams, "Sweet Dreams (Are Made Of This)" by Marilyn Manson echoes through the eerily empty club. I wouldn't say it's been a packed house any night since I've started working here, but it's definitely been fuller than this. Regardless of the number of people, I let myself get lost in the music, crawling to the end of the runway like I did during my first performance, and I'm ready to be disappointed again when I reach the edge and look up to see who's sitting there.

Only to look up and meet blue eyes.

The bulb lights from the perimeter of the stage barely illuminate his handsome face, but there's no mistaking it's him. My breath catches, my core heats, and my movements exaggerate slightly without my conscious thought. He stands unexpectedly, stepping to the side of the table he was sitting at and moving as close to me as the platform will allow. Unbidden, my back straightens and I rise, kneeling so our faces are almost level with each other.

His eyes drink me in while I sway on my knees, burning a path across my skin. I drop one hand from my hair and follow that molten path of sensation his gaze has created until I reach the apex of my thighs. Normally, I'd simply stop at a little over-the-clothes tease for some extra tips, but with his attention fixed there I can't help but be bolder than I ever thought I'd be capable of.

Ignoring everything outside of his presence, my fingers slowly slip under the waistline of my panties instead, and I can't help but gasp as they meet the wetness gathering there without my knowledge. A whimper escapes my lips, and Mr.

Conri's eyes snap up to meet mine as if he could hear the small noise over the thumping base. Shocked out of my momentary lapse in judgment I jerk my fingers out of my panties and start to retreat when his eyebrow cocks in a silent dare.

"Did I say you could stop?" his gaze seems to say.

I want to rise to his challenge, but what about the other patrons? I want to see who else is around and watching me, but I don't dare look away from him. This titan of a man has his full attention on me and I can't lose it.

All thoughts of rules, morals, and who else could be nearby become irrelevant in this moment. I slide my fingers slowly back under my panties and begin stroking my clit. My eyes slowly flutter closed as I begin rolling my hips with the pleasure I'm creating, but a growl reaches my ears as if he's right next to me and I snap back to attention. He hasn't moved from his spot in front of me, but I *swear* I felt his breath against my skin. The thought of him, hot breath against my neck, low, forceful growl reverberating within me, and the feelings of my fingers circling my clit push me into a frenzy.

I've never been able to orgasm before, but it feels like I'm about to for the first time. I always thought something was wrong with me. That I was missing something within me that made it impossible, or that I was just... well, wrong.

For the first time in my life, as I feel the pressure build under his heated gaze, I wonder if maybe I'm not missing something within myself after all.

Maybe I've just been missing *him*.

My breath stutters as I climb higher, forcing myself to maintain eye contact, hoping his strength will help bolster my own and finally allow me to fall over that final, shining cliff. The moment I reach the peak that I know is the goal, my alarm goes off.

I jolt awake, gasping for air and crying out in frustration when the tendrils of what was shaping up to be my first orgasm are violently shredded and float away on the waves of my disappointment.

"Noooo," I whimper, slapping the button on top of the clock to shut it up and slamming a pillow over my face to muffle my voice. "I was so close!"

Gran had several testing appointments today, which she begged me to skip since tonight is my first official night at The Den. I'm not sure why she's still trying to argue with me, she can't think it'll work! I took this job because it would allow me to make every appointment no matter what it is, so I'm not missing a single one.

She would do the same for me.

Heck, she has done the same thing for me my entire life. My mom died when I was young and she never knew who my father was, so it's always just been us. She's been there for me when no one else was. I'll do whatever I can to show her the same love and care she's always shown me.

Mina told me that I could keep some things at the club in a secured locker, so the amount of stuff I've got to take with me tonight is a bit ridiculous. I know Gran won't judge me for stripping since she used to do it too. That doesn't mean I want her to know about it, though, because she'll worry or feel more guilty than she already does. The last thing I want is to add to her stress right now, so I'm going to leave as much of the essentials at the club as I can. That means all of my stage makeup, hair tools and supplies, and stuff to wash my face or take a shower before I come home.

"Penelope," the same mountain man from my last visit greets me with a kind smile and a dip of his head. "Welcome back. That was quite a show you put on," he tells me, extending his huge hand to take my bags from me. "If my Mina has taught me anything, it's that anyone can shake it on stage. It takes true talent to look effortless on the pole."

My cheeks heat at the compliment. Normally I'd take what he's saying as a lecherous attempt to come on to me, but his easy smile, kind eyes, and the love with which he says Mina's name makes me think he's truly complimenting my athletic ability, not commenting on what I looked like without clothes on.

"Thank you," I respond quietly, handing over my bag. "You must be Mikey? Mina told me about you."

He huffs, trying to hide his pleasure in hearing she's mentioned him to me, but the pink tinge to the tips of his ears gives him away. Who would have thought that this scary looking man would be such a gentle giant? I certainly didn't. The door whines as he opens it and he gestures for me to precede him into the back hallway. I step inside and out of his way so he can take the lead once he's followed me in. I went in the front door the last time I was here, but as an employee I'm now coming in through the back entrance.

"Just Mike, actually," he says, much kinder with his correction than I was when we met. "Mina said you can take over the same vanity you used last time, and there's a new padlock in the package in the top drawer for your locker in case you didn't bring one. You won't go on for a few hours yet, so if you want to go work the floor and waitress you can head out when you're ready. Just a reminder, no lap dances on the first shift."

Mike gently places my bags on the floor next to the vanity I'll be using and when he steps away my brow furrows in confusion. There's a huge, stunning bouquet of crimson poppies in the center of the table.

"Mike?" I call out to him, "I think this is the wrong table? Someone else must be sitting here. I don't want to intrude on someone else's space."

He turns and grabs the card from the little stick it's perched on and hands it to me with a smile. "Nope. They're all yours. Good luck tonight, huh? If you get overwhelmed, find me or Mina. Anytime. You'll be safe, I promise." With that he pats the top of my head like I'm a little kid, which I guess compared to him I am, and exits the changing room while whistling a merry tune.

These may be the most beautiful flowers I've ever seen, but I don't understand. Gran wouldn't have sent them, and if Trevor did I'll have to nip that in the bud before it starts. No pun intended. I place my purse on the tabletop next to the bouquet and flip the card over to open the envelope. In a languid, flowing cursive is just one sentence.

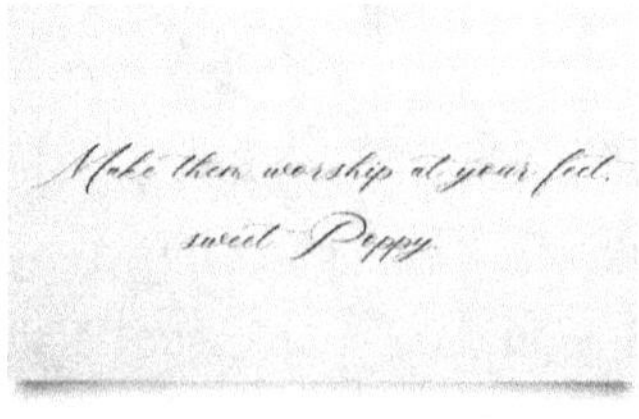

Chapter Five – Jager

Good.

My peace is interrupted by Felix and the cloud of desperation that always follows him. "Jager," he greets me, trying to act as if he's not the simpering fool he is. "May I?"

"You have ten minutes, Felix."

"Damnit, Jager," he curses as he takes a seat. "This is still my club!"

I can't help but scoff. "Is it? The deed may be in your name, but I own your ass. Fuck with me and I'll take everything."

"I pay my bills!"

"If you paid your bills we wouldn't be here, would we?" Mike asks, sidling up to the table and smirking at the delusional man.

"Fuck you, Mike," Felix snarls. "This isn't your business. Why don't you go distract Mina some more? It's not like she really does anything here, anyway."

"And lose the pleasure of your company? Why would I do that?"

"God damnit!"

"Enough!" I bark. "That's enough. Squabble later, I don't have the patience for it. Felix, I have lost faith in your ability to repay your loan. This place has become a pathetic shithole, and pathetic shitholes don't make money."

"We're doing fine, Jager."

"You're not. I was here when the house lights were on tonight and it's falling apart. The floors out here are disgusting, not to mention the private rooms. When you agreed to a loan from me, it was made very clear that I am a man who protects my investments. That means that I'm taking over."

"What? Trevor is managing things here just fine, Jager. I don't need you to-"

"Trevor can still play manager as long as he plays ball. No matter what, I'm going to shake things up around here. I've hired a team to do a deep clean tomorrow, and once we see what we're left with we'll be updating and redecorating. We need to pull the type of clientele that spends real money. The kind of clientele that her talent deserves." I nod in Penelope's direction as she enters the club proper and heads to the bar. "That woman will double the club's income, guaranteed."

"She's just a silly girl who's only here because Trevor has wanted her since high school."

"I'd watch your fucking mouth if I were you, man," Mike snaps, beating me to it. Felix is lucky, because my rebuke would have been much bloodier.

He's also lucky that a waitress has just popped up at the end of the table. "Hi Felix, can I get you the usual?"

It takes him a moment to answer because he's so focused on trying to intimidate Mike, but he finally just responds with a monotone, "Yeah."

"And you, Sir? What can I do for you?" I don't even bother looking at the woman since I know someone actually worthy of my attention is ascending the steps behind her.

"Nothing."

"Are you sure? I'm happy to serve you in *any* way possible."

There is nothing I want that this woman could give me.

"He's good," Mike answers for me as he shifts to the side, knowing I won't bother to respond to her again. "His order just got here."

Fuck.

Vibrant green eyes meet mine, and I'm filled with the same fire that sparked in me days ago. This woman is a force of nature, and Felix and Trevor need to get out of my way, because I will make this her fucking kingdom.

Penelope

I'm lost in thought, switching between finalizing my makeup and staring at the stunning flowers on my table when Mina sashays into the room.

"Hi, Sugar! Are you ready for your first night?"

"Hi!" I hop up from my stool and give her a quick hug. "I am. I think there's something wrong here, though. Mike said these flowers are for me, but they're addressed to someone named Poppy."

Her smile turns sly. "Oh, they're for you alright. I accepted the delivery myself."

"I don't... wait, is that my stripper name or something?" I panic, not loving that idea. I want to have at least some say in what I'm called here! "Oh my gosh, they're not from Trevor are they? Did he name me without asking? He knows I would not be ok with that!"

"No!" I think she can see the fear and worry in my eyes because she takes my hands and squeezes them gently. "No, Sugar. We'd never choose your stage name for you; don't worry about that. And they're not from Trevor, either, that little weasel." I choke out a laugh as my pulse slows a bit. "They're just from an admirer, that's all. You earned them after that last performance." She winks and spins me back to the mirror so I can continue getting ready. "Do you know what name you want to use? I'll need to tell the DJ before your set."

An admirer? I'm relieved to know they aren't from Trevor, but who else could it be? Certainly not Mr. Conri, right? I know he was there watching me, but I can't imagine a man like him would even consider giving me a second thought.

Shaking myself out of my reverie, I bite my bottom lip in consideration. "I don't know. I've been racking my brain but everything feels so... cliche."

"Hmm..." she ponders, picking up one of my curls and wrapping it around her finger. "How about Ruby? It matches your hair!"

I pull a tube of Ravish Me Ruby red lipstick out of my case and paint my lips to finish my makeup, then look at myself in the mirror. "Ruby," I muse. "I like it. Thanks Mina."

"No problem! Your waitressing uniform is in locker number 12. Since you're not doing lap dances yet it'll let the clientele know you're waitressing only while you're on the floor. Mikey and the other bouncers will be out there, so if anything funny happens just let one of them know and they'll handle it, ok? Do you have any questions?"

"No, I'm good. Thank you, Mina. You and Mike have both been amazing."

"That's what we're here for!"

"Somehow I doubt that, but I'll let it slide. I'll be ready in a jiff. Don't worry about me, I'll be fine."

"I know you will, Sugar," she insists, squeezing my shoulders and smiling. "Break a leg!"

My waitressing uniform is surprisingly modest, but I guess it makes sense if you want the attention to be on the dancers, since that's where the money is. It's a strapless black sheath that hits me mid thigh with thigh high fishnet stockings and a garter set. I brought a pair of black platform pumps with three inch heels for tonight, hoping that even though it's a bit higher than I usually prefer, my feet won't be killing me inside of five minutes.

Makeup done and hair fluffed, I take in my reflection in the floor length mirror and blink in surprise. I started avoiding wearing black after I was picked on for looking like a vampire when I was young, and I never really moved past it. I don't remember the last time, other than during my audition when I was nervous out of my mind, that I wore this much black and paid this much attention to my hair and makeup.

I'm a knockout!

I've never looked at myself and thought that before, but standing here in a strip club, dressed like I've always been afraid to dress, and getting ready to put my goodies on display for strangers?

I finally feel... beautiful.

Maybe I really *can* make them worship at my feet.

At the door to the club proper, I brace my hands on the metal surface and take a deep breath as I prepare to start my first shift. The bass pumps hard enough that I can feel it surge through my fingertips, and I sigh as I embrace the chaos I know is waiting on the other side. Refusing to hesitate any longer, I push against the bar on the door and step into my new reality.

To say the club looks different now than it did during my audition would be an understatement. The lighting is dim with a purple hue, hiding all of the flaws in the decor and making it look far better than it does when the house lights are on. Timberland is playing, and two women gyrate to the beat inside cages positioned on the two side stages. There are a few women giving customers lap dances and two waitresses flitting about trying to keep everyone else happy. Wanting to help, I hurry to the end of the bar where one of the two waitresses waits for her drinks. The bartender places one final glass on her tray and she grabs it up and walks away before I can introduce myself to her.

"Hi there," the bartender yells over the pumping music. "You're the new girl?"

"I am!" I holler back. "Pene- shoot!" I curse. "I'm Ruby!"

Her wide smile is infectious, a gap between her two front teeth adding to her beauty rather than detracting from it. "I'm Cassie!"

"Nice to meet you! Is there a list of tables for me, or do we just roam?"

"For the most part you'll just roam," she answers, pulling a crystal glass off the shelf behind her and dropping a perfectly square ice cube into it before filling it with a dark amber liquid. "Sometimes, though, a table will request you." Placing the filled glass on a napkin in the center of a circular tray, she slides it toward me. "Like this one."

"What?" I squeak. "I just got out here! I haven't talked to anyone yet." I look around frantically to see if I notice anyone familiar. No one other than Trevor knows I work here. Gran knows I have the job but not the name of the club. I don't see anyone watching me, but it's kind of dark so I can't see everyone here.

"It's his world, Ruby. We're just living in it."

"His? Who, Trevor?" Ugh! I really don't want to wait on him. Honestly, I know he runs the place and got me this job, but I'm worried he's going to use me being here as an excuse to try to get closer to me. He's a good guy; I'm just not interested in him. Especially with everything going on with Gran right now.

Her laugh is so bright and loud it's infectious. "Not a chance. That little fuck couldn't run a paper bag, let alone the world. Mina keeps this place going, no matter what Trevor tells you. This," she taps the tray right next to the glass, "is for our real boss. He's in the back corner over there."

I turn, following her pointed finger and while I can see the table she's pointing to, I can't see everyone seated. A large man stands in front of it, blocking all but one suit-clad arm of everyone except for Felix, who is leering at me from across the room. My stomach drops. Did he send the flowers? Afraid to show my absolute disgust since Cassie and Mina both seem to like him, I force a smile onto my face and turn back to her.

"Thank you, Cassie. I'll be back as soon as I can."

Cassie examines my face and can obviously see through my attempt, but she just smirks and winks. "You got this, Ruby. He's not as scary as he looks."

I take a deep breath and give her a real smile. I'm glad she hasn't had the same experiences with Felix that I have, and all she's doing is trying to help me relax on my first night. I nod my thanks and stiffen my spine as I start my walk across the club floor. I try to ignore Felix as I make my way toward him, but I can feel his eyes on me like disgusting, greasy, fumbling fingers. Instead of simply avoiding his gaze I make sure to offer smiles and greet the patrons seated at passing tables. I have to make sure that I do my job well no matter how uncomfortable I am. Not every man I'll interact with here will be handsome, respectful, and make me feel comfortable. I need to get used to working through these feelings.

I'm only steps away from the VIP section when a waitress practically sprints by me, running up the stairs and stepping up next to Felix who is seated at the end of the booth. I know we're in a strip club, but the desperate way she's arching her back so her boobs and butt stick out make it almost impossible to hold back the snort of laughter that bubbles up. She places a napkin on the table in front of Felix with a dramatic, low flourish, then caresses the table in what she probably thinks is a sensual way.

"Hi Felix, can I get you the usual?"

"Yeah." That's it? Just "Yeah?" What a jerk!

She takes it in stride though, and turns to the man still blocked by the wall of muscle in front of me. "And you, Sir? What can I do for you?"

"Nothing," a deep voice answers carelessly.

She stiffens at the rebuke, but obviously doesn't let it deter her. "Are you sure? I'm happy to serve you in *any* way possible." Her desperate emphasis on the word "any"" leaves me rolling my eyes.

"He's good," the mountain answers, turning to face me and revealing Mike's familiar face. "His order just got here."

His order? Not Felixes?

Oh, poop.

My heart stutters the moment Mike steps aside and reveals the beautiful, blue eyes that have been haunting my dreams — both waking and sleeping.

"But she just got here!" Rayne whines before turning to me with irritation. "How did you get his order? I've been waiting for it!"

"I..."

Not sure what to say I look to Mike for help. I don't want to fight with someone or make enemies on my first day! I didn't ask for this, I'm just doing what I'm told.

Mike scowls at Felix, who finally enters the conversation.

"Ranye," he snaps. "Just go. She's doing her job."

"But Felix! It's her first ni-"

"Leave."

The single word is barely loud enough to be heard over the beat of the music, but it's calm with an undertone of heat.

"But I-"

"Go!" Felix shouts, slamming his hand on the table.

Rayne and I both start at his outburst. She stamps her foot like a toddler then turns and runs, glaring at me as if this has all been my fault. She turns away too slowly, though, because I can easily see the tears rimming her eyes. I follow her movement and watch as she runs through the doors to the back of the club. I'll have to check on her later. Felix didn't have to be so mean to her!

"Hi, Penelope," Mike says, pulling my attention back to them.

"Hi, Mike. It's Ruby, actually." I smile and wink at him, thinking of the last time we met and I scolded him for getting my name wrong.

"Ruby, huh?" he says, looking me up and down with consideration instead of lust. "I like it. It's a little on the nose, but it suits you beautifully."

"Thank you," I respond, blushing. Working up my courage, I finally make eye contact with Mr. Conri again while lifting the drink from my tray. "Is this yours, Sir?"

"It is," he answers with a nod. "Thank you."

"Of course," I feel so tongue tied in front of him. I've never been attracted to an older man before, but something is drawing me to him, even if I feel almost like a child in comparison. "Felix, it looks like Rayne needs a moment. Would you like me to get your drink?"

"Felix was just leaving, actually."

Felix flinches back, surprised. "We're not done talking, Conri. We've got to nail out these details!"

"We're done for now. I need to speak with our new hire."

"Ours? Listen, Con-"

"Time to go, Felix," Mike tells him, stepping up to his side. "I'll call you back when you're wanted again."

"This is not how things are going to happen, Conri. You fucking bet we'll be discussing this later!"

Felix rises from his seat at the booth and stomps off, meeting Trevor where he's just entered the club from the door Rayne just went through. They look to be arguing, but who knows what it's about.

"I'm so sorry," I tell Mike and Mr. Conri, turning back to them. "I didn't mean to cause a problem. Mike, can I get you something?"

"Actually, Ms. Channing, would you please sit with me for a moment?"

"Me?" I squeak, surprised. Mike's laugh pulls a growl from me and I smack his stomach with the back of my hand. "Ouch!" I mutter, rubbing away the sting and coming back to myself when Mike roars a laugh so loud I can feel the collective attention of the club move to us. My heart stops when Mr. Conri stands and walks over, towering over me and gently taking my hand in his with a furrowed brow.

"Oh my goodness, I'm so-"

My words get caught in my throat when the beautiful man in front of me lifts my hand and places a gentle kiss on the spot where I smacked his friend. "Are you ok?" he asks, sincerity meeting my eyes while his lips are poised just above my skin.

"Ye- yes, Sir. I'm so sorry, I didn't mean to do that, I swear! Mike, I'm sorry! Did I hurt you?"

"Not at all, Ruby Red. Well, maybe my pride. Now all the other bodyguards are going to make fun of me for being beaten up by a tiny girl."

I can't help but scowl at him for making fun of me, but my attention returns to Mr. Conri when he straightens with a growl.

"Please, sit," he requests, leading me by the hand to take Felix's place at the table.

I look around the club, scanning the tables to see how full the customer's drinks are. There are several women out on the floor and most drinks seem full, so I take the risk and do as he asks.

"How long have you been dancing," he asks me, leaning back against the booth seat and taking a sip of the drink I brought him.

"How long?" I ask, trying to think of whether I should tell the truth or pretend it's been longer so I look more experienced. When he nods, I take a deep breath and sigh.

Like Gran says, always the truth.

"Technically, tonight is my first night."

"What do you mean, technically?"

"I've done pole work as an exercise routine for a while, but my first time in public was my audition."

"Really?" he asks, a single eyebrow raised in surprise.

"Yes, Sir."

"I was very impressed. You're a natural, and I enjoyed your choice of music."

"Thank you," I respond quietly, looking down to hide the blush that's brightening my cheeks. "I am sorry, but I do need to get back to work. I don't want to start on the wrong foot with my coworkers."

"I understand. Please bring me another before your next performance."

Chapter Six

"Gosh, Sugar. I still can't believe how good you are!" Mina gushes, hugging me as soon as I step off the stage. "I'd swear you've been at this for years. Mike told me the last time was your first performance! Was he teasing me?"

"No," I laugh. "I did it for exercise before with friends. I also used to dance ballet."

"Well, you're amazing." She links her arm with mine and leads me to the back. "And you have a guest in my office."

"Who?" I'm getting really tired of all of these surprises, it's overwhelming!

"Mr. Conri. He said he'd like to speak with you."

My step stutters, but I gather myself and shake off the nervousness. He's obviously a fixture here, if not possibly my boss's boss, so I need to get used to interacting with him. We reach her office and she shoos me in before winking and sashaying over to Mike who is waiting just down the hall.

"Mr. Conri?" I call, knocking on the door frame and stepping in to see him seated behind Mina's desk. "You asked to see me?"

"I did. That was another phenomenal performance, Penelope."

"Thank you, Sir."

He rises from the seat and walks around the desk to sit on the edge in front of me. "I'd like you to have dinner with me tomorrow."

"I'm sorry?"

"I have a dinner party to attend. It's usually rather boring, but I think it could be enjoyable with your company."

"I... well, I do appreciate the offer, but I can't."

"You're not working, I asked Mina to make sure."

"No, I'm not working. For one thing, I don't have anything I could wear."

Shoot, that wasn't supposed to be my first answer!

"That is easily remedied."

"My grandma is very ill and is starting treatment soon. I need to prepare her, and the house, and get a lot of things done. It's my only opportunity before treatment begins."

"What if I could get you some help?"

"That's very kind, but we can manage."

"Nonsense. I'll send my assistant tomorrow and she'll bring a dress with her as well."

"What? No, that's... I'm sorry, but I can't!"

"I'll see you at six, Miss Channing. Have a good night."

I try to form a response to his complete refusal to listen to the word *no*, but before I remember I can just say, "It's not going to happen, mister!" he's already gone.

Does he honestly think I'll go just because he said so? Surely not.

"Pen!" Gran yells, "Penny get up! There's someone at the door and I'm washing dishes!"

"Wha–?" I mutter, struggling to lift my head from the pillow and focus on the time shining from my bedside clock. It's only nine a.m.! I've barely gotten a few hours of sleep.

"Penelope Grace Channing you get your lazy butt up and get that door!"

"Ugh!" I throw the covers off and snatch my robe from the floor, stumbling out of my room and down the hall to the front door of our little home. I open the door, squinting at the light that shines brightly behind our visitor.

"'llo?"

I can't quite see who it is, so I shield my eyes as best I can. A lovely young woman stands on the doorstep with an apologetic smile on her face, wincing when she realizes I've just left my bed.

"I'm so sorry, Ms. Channing. I know you worked late last night—"

"You do?"

"But you've got a full day ahead of you and I don't want you to miss a minute!"

"I do?"

Her excited tone turns to concern when she asks, "Did he not tell you? He said you knew!"

"He said?"

"Mr. Conri. He said you'd be expecting us."

"Expecting you?"

My brain must still be asleep because I can't seem to form full sentences. Thankfully, a hand appears in front of me from the side and I happily accept the mug of coffee offered.

"You'll have to forgive my granddaughter. She isn't human until she's had a cup of coffee."

She isn't wrong.

"How can we help you, Miss?"

"No problem!" she giggles. "I'm Mika. And we're here to help you, actually." The woman turns and points to a team of people standing behind her that I completely missed.

Oops.

"My understanding is Ms. Channing mentioned that you both have a lot going on right now and we wanted to help. We have deep cleaning and organization specialists here to take care of your home, and there's a car waiting there," she points to the large SUV parked at the end of the driveway behind the work vans, "to take you both to the spa for a day of treatments and relaxation."

"Who is *we*?" Gran asks, looking at me with skepticism. "Penny, did you get one of those... those candy people at the club you're waitressing at? What were you thinking?"

"What?" I sputter, wincing as coffee spouts from my lips. "What the heck is a candy person?"

"You know, the ones who give you money when you give them... candy. Of the carnal type."

"Gran! What the heck? No!"

"No, Ma'am!" Mika laughs, covering her mouth slightly and thankfully backing me up. "Mr. Conri is an owner of the club where Ms. Channing works. When he heard of the troubles you were experiencing he wanted to help. He also sent this for you," she finishes, handing me a card.

"What does it say?" Gran asks.

I pause to look at Gran, incredulous. "Does it look like I've opened it yet? Here." I hand her my cup of coffee and turn the envelope over. I'm surprised to find a wax seal keeping it closed. It's a crimson that matches the exact shade of my hair, and the stamp in the center is an image of a howling wolf. It's stunning.

I carefully pry the flap open, careful to keep the seal intact so I can put it in my keepsake box later, and remove a thick white piece of cardstock with a handwritten note. It's in the same elegant script as the note that came with my flowers.

> Penelope,
> Please provide me the pleasure of your company for dinner tonight. It truly will be dull without you there to brighten things up.

My first reaction is relief that he didn't call me Poppy since Gran is reading it over my shoulder, the second is a storm of butterflies taking flight in my stomach. He's doing all of this just so I'll have dinner with him?

Is this too much? This refusal to accept my rejection? Is this one of those red flags I've heard so much about?

Do I care?

"Hmph," Gran mutters. "A spa day, you said?"

Spa day was an understatement, unless this is simply how the one percent lives. We were massaged, soaked, plucked, primped, polished, trimmed, styled, and made up. They even did a special treatment on Gran's hair to help protect it from the harsh chemicals she'll undergo with the chemo. Everyone was so kind, and we both looked absolutely beautiful by the time we left.

When we got home though? I realized that the real work was done there.

Every inch of the house was scoured clean. Gran always keeps things neat and tidy, but now they shine like new. Every room in the house has been completely organized, and the fridge and freezer stocked with prepared meals, snacks, and drinks that will easily feed both of us for days. The food all looks delicious and healthy, most of it safe for Gran's stomach while going through treatment.

The team even left a note on the counter.

Channing Family,

We hope you are satisfied with the services you received today! Mr. Conri has contracted our services moving forward as well. Cleaners will come twice per week, and food will be delivered once per week. Please call the number below with your preferred days and times, and any food requests so that we can make sure you have whatever you need! If you have need for us to come more frequently, whether on a regular schedule or for last-minute assistance, that has been authorized. Simply call and we will arrange it.

We look forward to helping take care of you through this journey!

I've been so worried about how I was going to juggle everything — taking care of Gran during and after her appointments, cooking, cleaning, and working. I wouldn't change being able to do all of this for the world, but the stress of it was starting to take a toll and treatment hasn't even started!

"Gran!" I gasp, showing her the card as tears well in my eyes. "We can't accept this, right? It's too much!"

"Does he do this for all of his employees?" Gran asks Mika, eyes wide in shock.

"No, Ma'am," she answers solemnly. "Mr. Conri is a very generous man, but this is a bit out of the ordinary."

"We have to tell him we can't accept this. Mika, can you please tell him? He didn't listen to me when I tried to tell him no!"

"I'm sorry, Ms. Channing, but that's a bit above my paygrade. You can tell him tonight, though."

"I can't! I still don't have a dress or anything! This is insane." I look frantically from Mika to Gran. "It's insane, right?"

"Hush, Penny. You're fine, sweetheart. The least you can do is thank the man in person; his kindness today cost a fortune. I'm sure we have something you could wear."

"If you'll follow me, actually, I have something for you."

I sigh, nervous as heck and placing the note back on the kitchen counter before following her to my room. Everything looks perfect, my bed is even made for the first time since I moved back home, and there's a gorgeous charcoal gray off-shoulder bodycon dress hanging on the closet door with a pair of black heels and matching purse placed perfectly beneath it.

"Oh Penny, it's beautiful," Gran breathes, stepping up to the dress to feel the fabric and pick up one of the shoes to examine it closer.

Was that...

"Mika?" I whisper, heartbeat in my throat. I don't want Gran to hear me ask this question because she has no idea what she's holding.

"Yes?" she whispers back.

"Are those what I think they are?"

"They are." She smiles softly, seeming to understand that I'm kind of freaking out.

Red soles.

I've never even been in the same room as red soled shoes. And now I'm supposed to *wear* them?

It's official — I'm in way over my head.

Chapter Seven

Tonight was so incredibly wonderful. Every time nerves started to get the best of me Mr. Conri was there with a smile, a soft and reassuring touch, or guiding the conversation in such a way that I was able to join without feeling like I was completely out of my league. The food was delicious, and the outfit he provided fit perfectly, making me look like a more mature version of myself.

He's a complete gentleman — insisting upon opening doors, helping with my chair, and never allowing me to feel left out. Now we're back at my place, and after learning at the restaurant that I wasn't supposed to open my own car door, I wait patiently while he exits the expensive vehicle and opens it for me from the outside. I accept the hand extended to me and turn in my seat as elegantly as possible so I can get down. His SUV is so tall I need assistance both getting in and out. Instead of allowing me to use his hand for support as I try to climb down this time, however, he drops it and uses my moment of surprise to wrap his large hands around my waist. Grip strong but gentle, he lifts me up high enough to ensure our bodies brush as he lowers me to my feet.

His chest is rock hard. My breath hitches when my breast passes over his nipple, because even though I can't be sure, I think I feel the brush of a metal piercing.

"Thank you," I whisper, blushing and looking down.

"It was my pleasure," he answers quietly, lifting my chin to force me to meet his gaze. "Thank you for joining me this evening."

"You didn't really give me a choice, did you?" I try to force a laugh, still unsure if I feel like it was the right thing to do.

"No."

His answer is short and completely unapologetic. Just, no.

"I didn't get to say this earlier, but as much as I appreciate everything from today you can't keep doing it. It's too much!"

"It's not up for discussion."

"Yes, it is!" I argue, my fire finally coming out. He makes me nervous, but this is important.

"No, it's not. If for no other reason than it's an investment. If you're worried about your grandmother you won't be dancing with your full focus. I need you dancing with your full attention, because you're going to be headlining."

"Headlining?" I yelp.

"Headlining. Besides, you deserve all of it and more."

"I just... it's just too much. You don't even know me."

"I know enough."

"You don't! All you know right now is that I'm a good dancer with a relatively pretty face."

"Don't ever talk about yourself like that," he snaps, making me jump as his grip tightens slightly around my chin. "I may not know much, but I know that you are kind, caring, and thoughtful. You always want to make sure the people around you are comfortable and taken care of, and while you bloom under that spotlight, you want to keep none of it for yourself. No matter how much you deserve it."

I'm stunned. No one has ever said anything about me like that. I blink slowly, taking in everything he just said.

"Thank you," I whisper, a single tear slipping down my cheek. Before he can say anything else I stand up on my toes and press a soft kiss to the corner of his mouth. I turn and run away, grabbing my keys from my purse as I make it to the front door.

I think I'm in trouble.

"You really don't need to go out of your way for me," I insist, nervous of what he'll think of me when he sees my old car. Dinner last night proved Mr. Conri is a man who has a lot of money, and while my baby is reliable, he's definitely not a looker.

It was my mom's car, and though Gran didn't have the money to make sure the paint stayed fresh, she always made sure to keep it in good running condition, and so have I. "Harvey and I will be just fine."

It takes a few seconds for me to realize that I'm the only one still walking.

"Mr. Conri?" The look of anger on his face surprises me. What happened to change his mood so quickly? "Is everything ok?"

"Who in the fuck is Harvey?"

"What?"

"I said, 'Who. The fuck. Is Harvey?'"

It takes me a second to realize what I'd said. My laugh rings out louder than I've let it in a long time, this one misunderstanding removing the last of the stress and nerves from my system. I practically skip up to his side and link my arms with his. "Come on, I'll introduce you."

"Penelope, who the fuck is Harvey? Do you have a boyfriend waiting for you?"

"No!" I giggle, pulling him around a corner and pointing at the car directly in front of us. I immediately peer up at him to gauge his reaction, and I'm so glad I did. "Get it? His name is Harvey."

"You named your car Harvey? Why?"

"Well, technically his full name is Harvey Dent," I tell him, waiting for the lightbulb to switch on.

...And waiting.

"Don't you get it?"

Frustration and honest confusion are my only response. I sigh.

"Harvey Dent from Batman. He's Two Face. Do you see it yet?" I continue to watch his face while he takes in my car once more, smiling as the realization sinks in.

"Harvey, huh?" he chuckles. Chuckles! "That's a good one."

I beam at him, sidling up next to my car and running a hand along the surface of the roof on the driver's side. We still can't figure out what happened or why, but for some reason the paint on only one half of the car dried out, cracked, and peeled almost completely off. That means the left side of the car from the grill to the back bumper looks like it's been beaten to death, while the right half looks almost pristine.

Thus, the name Harvey.

"You cannot drive this death trap," he grunts, shaking his head in disgust.

"Shh!" I scold, jumping to cover as much of the sideview mirror as I can as if the car has ears. "You'll hurt his feelings. I'll have you know Harvey is in perfect working order! He's never let me down. He never let my mom down, either!"

Instead of a verbal response, I simply receive a raised brow.

Challenge accepted.

I unlock the door and drop into the driver's seat, smiling cheekily as I insert the key and attempt to start the car

Nothing.

A dark smile spreads over his face and mine drops. No matter what I do, the car won't turn over! I pop the hood and try to check the engine, but Mr. Conri stops me.

"Penelope, I'm not even going to tell you I told you so. I'm just going to drive you home and have my mechanic fix the issue."

"No! I can't let you do that!"

"Penny?"

Ugh! Freaking Trevor!

I turn and scowl at him, annoyed at Mr. Conri's insistence that he fix my car, embarrassed that the one time I was fully confident Harvey would pull through he failed, and exasperated that Trevor refuses to respect my boundaries concerning my name. "Trevor, you need to stop calling me that!"

"Sorry," he winces, moving up next to Mr. Conri. "Is everything ok?"

"Nothing you need to concern yourself with."

I scowl at Mr. Conri and force a smile for Trevor. "It's fine, Trevor. Thank you. Just an issue with my car."

"Oh, no! Do you want me to take a look?"

"No, thank you. I'm sure it's fine."

"I can at least give you a ride home, it's on my wa—."

"Not happening," Mr. Conri interjects

"Excuse me?" Trevor wants to sound confident in his rebuttal, but standing next to Mr. Conri, he looks like an emaciated teenager.

"I said, it's not happening. I'll be taking her home."

"I didn't ask you!" Trevor insists, indignant. "You can't answer for her!" Great. Maybe he'll stomp his foot like a toddler to complete the effect.

"I just did."

"Trevor," I interrupt, not wanting them to get into an argument. "Thank you for the offer, but I've already accepted a ride from Mr. Conri. I'll be ok, and I'll see you tomorrow, alright?"

"Are you sure?"

"Of course. Thank you for your offer, though. Have a good night, Trevor."

He looks from me to Mr. Conri, then simply shakes his head and walks off, fists at his side like a petulant child.

"Yikes," I wince. "I'm so sorry about that, but I promise he means well. I couldn't ask you to go so far out of your way, though. It's an hour-long drive. Thank you so much for the offer, but I'm happy to take an Uber home."

"Absolutely not." He lifts the hood of the car just enough to be able to drop it closed again, then steps into the roadway and lifts a hand, calling for a waiting car to pull up.

Chapter Eight

The car that pulls up in front of us is a sleek, black SUV with darkly tinted windows. Mr. Conri directs me to the rear passenger door with a warm hand at the small of my back, opening the door and assisting me in climbing up into the seat, closing the door once I'm safely seated. While my escort makes his way around the back of the car to take his own seat I meet the eyes of the driver in the rearview mirror. I smile and greet him, but all I receive is a solemn nod in response.

Once Mr. Conri takes his seat next to me, he provides the driver my address.

Wait, he has it memorized? I can't decide if that's overbearing or sexy, but considering the heat that just flared between my thighs I'm guessing the latter.

The driver keys it into the dashboard navigation system, then mutters a quiet curse. "It looks like there's an accident on the highway, Sir. Right now it's saying it'll take about two hours to get there."

"Oh my gosh!" I gasp. "No way! That's way too inconvenient, please let me call an Uber." Mr. Conri simply nods his approval and hits a button on the side of his door, causing a partition to begin slowly rising between us and the driver. "Mr. Conri, please."

"Jager," he says quietly, causing the driver to jerk in place. His dramatic movement drew my attention and I meet his wide eyes in the rearview mirror for mere moments before the barrier separates us completely.

"I'm… sorry?"

He reaches over and clasps my hand, pulling it to him and rubbing his thumb over the top. "Call me Jager."

"Oh. Ok." Is that not normal? I want to ask, but the way the driver reacted makes it pretty obvious it isn't. "Jager, I can't ask that of you! It's so incredibly inconvenient."

"You're not asking," he says calmly, watching the path his thumb takes and smirking when he realizes my skin has broken out in goosebumps. "I'm insisting."

A shiver shocks through my system, and I realize I don't want to say no to him. Gathering my courage, I raise my gaze to meet his beautiful eyes. "Thank you, Jager."

"Of course. It's my pleasure."

I don't know what to say, so I just sit in bashful silence. I've been on dates with boys in the past and have even spent time alone in a car with them. But those... those were *boys*.

This is a man.

A man who seems to see something in me. Is that really possible?

Silence surrounds us, but it's not strained at all. It is, however, chilly in here. I didn't bring my jacket tonight because Harvey always runs so warm, but the air conditioning in this luxury car works well enough that I'm soon shivering.

"Are you cold?" he asks, breaking the silence and startling me.

"A little," I admit, not wanting to inconvenience him any further than I already have. He's driving two hours to take me home; he doesn't need to be uncomfortable the whole time, too!

"Come here."

"Wh– what?"

"Come here, Penelope."

Releasing my hand, he unbuckles my seatbelt and pulls me toward him. I scoot over, thinking he wants me to sit next to him, but I release a squeal of surprise when grips my waist and lifts me onto his lap with my back against the door. Surprisingly, our bodies are perfectly aligned, my small frame to his muscular build, and I know if I lean my head against him it will fit perfectly against his shoulder. I'm so tempted to see if I'm right, but while he may feel comfortable taking liberties, I can't gather the courage.

As time wears on, the silence combined with the warmth of Jager's body lulls me into a contented, sleepy state. My focus is completely centered on the heat of his palm through the fabric of my skirt, and I can't help but finally allow my head to droop sleepily until it's nestled into the crook of his neck, fitting just where I imagined it would. A pleased rumble vibrates through his chest, and his fingers slowly tighten against my thigh, causing my breath to catch as he begins slowly massaging the area.

"Is this ok?" he asks, his voice so low and quiet it's almost guttural.

I hesitate for a moment, wondering if this is a good idea. If I'd be the same person after allowing this man to touch me.

I'm so worried about Gran. And money. And my car, and how I'll do at my new job, and if I'll ever be able to finish school.

I don't want to worry about wanting something that may or may not be good for me, too.

I nod.

He releases my thigh and gently grasps my chin, tilting my face up to meet his waiting gaze. "Use your words. Tell me, Sweet Poppy. Yes, or no?"

"Yes."

"Good girl." Leaning forward, he presses a brief kiss to the corner of my mouth and caresses my cheek with his thumb before guiding my head back to rest against him again. His palm skims down my neck, arm, and down my thigh to my knee. I sigh and melt into him as he begins a gentle and sensual massage, working his way from my knee up the inside of my thigh. I've messed around with guys before, but his touch is unlike anything I've ever felt. It's purposeful and confident. There's no desperate, awkward fumbling or rush to get into my panties to prove how easily they can make me come.

Not-so-fun fact? They never can.

When his hand reaches the hem of my skirt he pauses with the tips of his fingers just underneath.

"Tell me."

It feels crazy, but for once I really don't care.

"Yes," I sigh against his skin, surprising both myself and him by opening my legs slightly wider for him.

Again, I expect him to immediately slip his fingers under my panties, but he simply continues his slow, sensual massage. The buildup is causing what I assume is his intended goal. My breath is becoming labored, my body growing warmer by the moment, and at this point he's so close to my apex I'm almost ready to beg for him to touch me where I need him.

Minutes of beautiful torture pass before I give in to my desire. I slide my hand up his chest so I can grip his shirt and spread my legs a bit wider, tilting my hips in invitation.

"Please," I whisper when his finger finally brushes against the fabric of my panties. I'm half afraid to look like a pathetically desperate little girl, and half realizing that's what I may actually be. Also maybe another half not caring if that means I get what I want.

I definitely don't care if the math doesn't add up.

I'm afraid my fear has been realized when he suddenly removes his hand from where I want it, but he simply clasps my chin and uses his grasp to pull my lips to his before returning his fingers to my core once more.

His kiss is just as sensual and confident as his hands are. My eyes flutter shut, allowing me to focus on the sensations of what he's doing to me. When he finally slips his fingers past the edge of my panties I whimper and push harder against his hand and mouth, surrendering to my desperation for him. Moments later, he slips one finger inside me. The surprise of it finally happening pulls a gasp from me and allows him to slide his tongue between my parted lips.

He tastes like smoke and whiskey, and between his touch and his flavor, I feel like I'm getting drunk on him alone. His tongue mimics the movement of his finger, sliding expertly in and out of me while his stubble pricks against my skin. I always thought stubble would be painful or abrasive, but it's just one more reminder that this man is just that — a man.

The warmth building in my core is that same feeling I've experienced a hundred times, more often alone than with a boyfriend. I'm fully ready to traverse this same old plateau, happy to just be in this moment with him.

It may be enough for me, but apparently it's not enough for him.

My grip on his shirt tightens as his hand rotates, slipping another finger inside me before bending them slightly. The combination of pressure from his thumb on my clit and his thick fingers moving in and out of me almost short circuits my brain, and for the first time ever I feel myself climbing higher than ever before.

Jager

Sweet little Poppy is curled up on my lap, clinging to my shirt, and rocking against my hand as if my touch is her salvation. I had no intention of seducing her when I insisted on driving her home, but the moment she shivered I knew I had a choice. My options were to give her my jacket or provide her with warmth in a more... intimate and satisfying way.

Turning up the heat simply wasn't an option. She'd be surrounded by me in one way or another.

Her body stutters when I adjust the position of my hand, adding a second finger and applying pressure to her clit. She tenses slightly, her kiss slowing as a faint tremor begins spreading throughout her body.

"Wait," she pants, pulling away from me and wrapping her fingers around my wrist to pull my hand back. "Something's wrong!"

Panic has widened her eyes and I reluctantly allow her to remove my touch from her sweet heat.

"What?" I ask, glancing down at my fingers to ensure she isn't bleeding. "What's wrong?"

"I... I don't know!" She whimpers, turning away from me and dashing a tear away from her cheek. "I'm sorry, Jager. Something is wrong with me."

I stop her attempt to slide off my lap with an arm around her waist and gently direct her gaze back to mine. "Nothing is wrong with you. What's going on?"

"I think... I think I'm broken."

"Broken?" I scoff, then pull myself together when I see her wince of pain at my disdain. She misread me. I'm not scoffing at her, I'm scoffing at the idea that anything could be wrong with this beautiful creature. "Tell me what you think is wrong. What do you think is broken?"

"I don't know," she whispers, closing her eyes to hide the pain that is so evident in them.

"Tell me," I urge, my voice much softer now.

"I can't orgasm!" she blurts. Her eyes pop wide and she slaps a hand across her mouth as she realizes what she just admitted. I pause, my mouth slightly open as I try to decide how to answer her. "See?" she asks, voice muffled for a moment until she removes her hand again. "There's something wrong with me. I should have told you before. I'm so sorry, Jager." Her eyes are welling with tears, causing my temper to spike. Why would she feel so broken if someone didn't make her feel this way?

"Why?" I ask her, voice calm and quiet.

"Why what?"

"Why should you have told me?"

"Because..." she pauses, shrugging. "It would have saved you some time."

"Listen to me," I grip her chin gently and force her to meet my sure gaze so she can see I mean every word I'm saying. "There is nothing, absolutely *nothing*, wrong with you. You are not broken, and I'll kill anyone who says otherwise." Her eyes widen at my statement, but I refuse to take back something I mean wholeheartedly. "You are beautiful," I press a soft kiss to her lips, "and sexy," this kiss to her jaw, "and from the moment I saw you I knew you would be absolutely addictive."

Her eyes are watering again, but it's no longer from fear or embarrassment. "But what if I never can?"

"I'm not worried about that," I insist, guiding her to shift on my lap so she's sitting with her back to my chest. I lean my head closer, trailing my nose from her neck to her ear and whisper, "Because I won't stop trying until you do." Once she's positioned correctly I wrap one arm around her chest and hold her to me as I toggle the button to recline my seat back as far as it will go. I slowly slide my hand up her sternum until I can cup her throat, tilting her head to the side. I lick and nip at the spot where her neck meets her shoulder, then kiss up her neck and back to her ear. I tighten my grip on her neck ever so slightly to make sure she's paying attention. "I won't stop until you are absolutely sated."

Her breathing is labored at this point, and I know I've gotten her exactly where I want her.

"Tell me, Sweet Poppy."

"Yes," she whispers. "Yes, please."

"Spread your legs for me, and lift your skirt."

After a moment's hesitation, she does as instructed. The shift of her hips grinds her ass against my hard cock, but knowing this will be her first orgasm makes any thought of my own a distant concern.

She is so far from broken, and I'm going to prove that shit to her right fucking now.

Once she's in position she allows her head to drop back against my chest. I skim the fingers of my free hand down her stomach to the waistband of her panties and begin to tease the skin underneath.

"Watch the stars, little one," I whisper against her skin. "Let go of yourself and let me show you how perfect you really are."

Her entire body shudders against me as I slip beneath the fabric of her panties. My fingers glide between her lips so easily it pulls an unexpected grunt from me, which turns into a low groan when her pussy greedily welcomes my fingers once more. This time, there's no taking it slow. I'm going to prove to her I can and will give her everything.

Poppy slowly begins to match my rhythm, rolling her hips against me and grinding down on my cock as she rides my fingers.

"Good girl," I croon quietly into her ear, "take what you need."

I try to push deeper within her, but my watch band gets caught on her panties.

"These need to come off. Do you want to do it, or should I help?"

"Huh? Off?" she asks, her voice hazy and thick with lust.

"Off."

"Um... help."

Without hesitation, I grip both sides of her underwear and tug, ripping them apart. Instead of the shocked gasp I'm expecting, however, the action elicits a low, drawn out moan.

"It's time to come for me, Poppy." I widen my own legs and brace against the floorboard so I can spread her further and guide her to brace her feet on my knees. "Close your eyes."

She follows my instruction without question, lifting a hand to run her fingers through my hair and nuzzle against my neck. While her eyes are closed I reach over to the center console control panel and flip the switch to change the moon-roof from transparent glass to a mirrored reflection. Seeing her spread out over top of me is bewitching. The pair of us are all black clothes and pale skin, and her crimson locks are splayed across us like a shock of fresh blood.

Fucking stunning.

Easing my fingers back inside her, I wrap my free hand around her tender throat once more. There's no need for me to tighten my grip yet, but I want her to get used to my hand being there. Her throat, just like her pussy, is mine.

I'm going to claim her first orgasm, and soon I'm going to claim her.

A whimper draws my attention back from my plans for the future, and her body is once again shaking. Her eyes are clenched so tightly shut that her forehead and nose are creased with the effort. She looks to be in pain, and that's unacceptable. This is all about pleasure.

"Open your eyes and look up," I command, ready to meet her gaze in the mirrored image. Her gasp is one of confusion, but again, that hip roll intensifies.

"That's right," I hum. "Does this stunning body look broken to you?" When she doesn't answer I give in to my impulse and tighten my grip slightly around her throat. "Tell me."

"No."

"Good. Now, watch me make you come."

I pump my fingers in and out of her pussy and release her throat so I can play with her clit as well. Her muscles begin tensing even further and her back bows against me as she continuously whispers, "Please, please!"

"Look at you, so fucking beautiful splayed out on top of me. So desperate for the release you deserve, and only I can give you. Your pussy takes my fingers so perfectly, Poppy. I think the only thing better will be when you take my cock."

"Co-" she stutters. "Your cock?"

"Of course. Do you want my cock, sweet girl?" I pull my fingers out slowly and spread her lips so she can see herself in the overhead mirror. "Do you want me to fill you so deeply that you're not sure where you end and I begin? Because I want that.

"Come for me, Poppy. Prove to me that I can give you what you need, and I'll give you everything you want."

"You want that?" Poppy pants. "I don't understand."

"There's nothing to understand. I was drawn to you the moment I saw you, I wanted you as soon as I watched you dance, and I needed you as soon as we met.

Why do you think I call you Poppy? You're like a fucking crimson drug that I don't want to ignore."

I twist my wrist slightly and crook my finger at a new angle, then press down on her clit. The sudden change was exactly what she needed, because she fucking detonates. The walls of her pussy pull my fingers in further and her back arches as she shouts her release. It takes several seconds for her to calm and catch her breath, but once she finally does she rolls over in place and snuggles against me.

"I don't want to ignore you, either," she whispers. "Thank you, for showing me I'm not broken."

"Even if you were, broken is beautiful, too."

Her contented sigh as she presses a kiss to my chest puts the final nail in my coffin.

I wasn't lying, this woman is addictive.

And no matter what, she's mine.

Chapter Nine

I've been up for hours and I'm starting to get worried — how do I get my car back? Is it really being worked on, or is it still at the club? As I scroll through my phone, debating on whether I should text Mina to ask her about it, a knock sounds at our front door.

"Who is it?" Gran asks, not even looking up from her English Muffin.

"Gran, if I were psychic we'd be in a completely different place right now," I grumble, making my way down the front hall to find out. I peek through the peephole and am somewhat surprised to find Mike standing there with a big, friendly smile.

"Hey, Mike," I greet as I open the door. I look past him to see if Jager is there, but there's no sign of him, just a motorcycle parked at the end of the driveway and another man jumping up into a lifted truck before it pulls away. My car is also here, looking suspiciously clean.

Are those new tires?

"Hey, Penelope. Hopefully this isn't too early?"

"Are those new tires?" I groan, glaring at him. What the heck?

"Don't shoot the messenger!" he defends, holding his hands up in surrender. "I told him you'd be pissed but he didn't listen to me. It was all I could do not to get him to 'accidentally' junk it."

"No way!"

"Yes, way," he laughs. It's fleeting, though, because he soon turns serious. "Listen, there's a reason he wanted to junk it."

"You mean besides the obvious?" I gesture to Harvey, Vanna White style.

"Actually, yes. It looks like the engine was tampered with, which is why it wouldn't start. There was a tracker on there, too."

"What?" my frantic yelp finally draws Gran's attention.

"What's wrong, Penny?" she asks, brow furrowed in concern.

"Mike said my engine has been messed with, and they found a tracker!"

"What? Who would do that?"

"We don't know, Ma'am, but we're going to look into it. In the meantime, we'd like to offer you both transportation until we do."

"Absolutely not!" I snap, wincing when I realize I'm directing my anger in the wrong place. "Sorry, Mike, but as much as I appreciate it, that's too much. We have functioning vehicles and are fully capable of taking care of ourselves."

"Don't be hasty, dear."

"Pardon?"

Gran can't actually be thinking about accepting this, can she? He's already done too much for us!

"Hear me out, Penny," Gran pleads. "If someone is messing with your car, there's no telling what else they have planned. I would feel safer if you were being watched over."

"Gran, you can't be serious! This is too much!"

"Your safety isn't too much, Penelope," Mike interjects.

"Listen to the man!" Gran chuckles. "If nothing else, it will ease my mind when you're working late at night. Please, Penny?" she pleads with me. "Just until they figure out who is behind it."

"Fine," I growl. "But only until then. And I swear to goodness, Mike, if he drags this out just so I'll keep accepting rides I'll... I'll..."

"You'll what?" he asks, a smirk creasing his stupid, handsome face.

"I'll make him wish he never met me!"

"Noted."

JAGER

"What the hell do you think you're doing, Jager?"

Felix's nephew has lost his fucking mind if he thinks I'm going to allow him to speak to me like that. Instead of ripping into him, however, I just stare at him with a complete lack of interest. This kid is less than nothing to me.

"I asked you a question!"

"And I'm choosing not to fucking answer."

"I'm not kidding, Jager. I want to know what you're thinking. Penny is a sweet girl, she's innocent! You need to leave her the fuck alone."

"First of all," Mike interjects before I can stab the little fuck in the throat. "I know you know her name is Penelope. I know she's told you probably a thousand fucking times that she doesn't like it when you call her Penny, but you seem to be incapable of listening. Show the woman some respect. Especially if you're going to pretend to care about her so much."

"I care about her more than you could poss–"

"Second, it's Mr. Conri to you. You haven't earned the right to speak to him as if you're colleagues."

"What is it that you want, kid?" I ask, smirking at his obvious anger and the way his eye twitches when I call him a kid.

"I want you to leave Pen... elope... alone. She's a sweet girl. She's innocent. She's going through a lot and she doesn't need you to make things worse for her!"

"What I do or do not do with her," I answer quietly, "or anyone else for that matter, is none of your fucking concern."

"Don't give me that! Her fucking grandmother has cancer and is probably dying! I gave her this job because she needs to work to make money for her care —me! They've always struggled for money, the medical bills are going to be piling up, and you monopolizing her time while she's here is just going to make things worse for her! You don't know what it was like growing up for her. She–"

Wham.

Thud.

Mike's fist came out of nowhere, surprising even me. Satisfaction hits me when Trevor hits the ground, looking up to me in dazed confusion with blood dripping out of his nose.

"I don't know who you think you are," Mike says, "but from this moment on you will keep your nose in your own fucking business. You will not spread her and her grandmother's personal information around. If they want to share that with people, they will. I'd be less worried about Jager monopolizing her time and more worried about Penelope beating your ass once she finds out you're talking out of turn."

It used to piss me off when Mike would step in before I could, but now I just roll with it. He's a good man with a better heart than mine, and sometimes it's scarier to not have to move a muscle to make a point. As Trevor struggles to his feet and scurries away like a little bitch, I'd wager he got the point.

If not? Well, let's just say I already have my eye on him.

Penelope

I place the usual drink on the table and stiffen my spine as I prepare to attempt to make Jager see reason. I know we've gotten somewhat intimate… ok really intimate, but that doesn't mean he can just take over my life! I can take care of Gran and myself. I'll make it work on my own.

Right?

"Listen, Jager," I'm stopped by the gasp of everyone around us and look at them all frantically. Oh, no! Was I not supposed to call him that in public? "I mean, Mr. Conri-"

"Jager."

Leaning close so I can speak quietly enough that only he can hear me I ask, "Are you sure?"

He simply nods and takes a sip of the drink I brought him. "Ok," I sigh. "I appreciate everything you're doing for me, but it's just too much! I can't accept all of this."

"You can, and you will."

"But-"

"We can discuss this later. Over dinner."

"Absolutely not!"

More gasps, and this time, a few snickers.

"Fine. Breakfast."

"Ugh! I have to work now. But you're right, we will discuss this later!"

His smirk is sexy as heck and incredibly infuriating.

"I look forward to it."

I turn and stomp off, but I'm called back to the table by a single word.

"Poppy."

Stopping dead, I turn and narrow my eyes at him in warning.

"Yes?"

"You forgot your tip."

He's holding up a hundred dollar bill. I start to get irritated, but then I smile. Adding a little sway to my walk, I saunter back up to his table and snag the money from his extended fingers. "Thank you, Sir," I say sweetly. "But now you have a choice to make. You can either tip me for my service, or we can have that discussion later. It's up to you." I show him the cash then tuck it into the top of my garter before turning to walk away. Looking over my shoulder I raise a single eyebrow — courtesy of Gran spending hours teaching me when I was young. "I'll hold onto this until you make your decision."

I practically skip away while Mike laughs uproariously and I store the surprised look on his face in my favorite memories.

Is this what power feels like?

Because I like it.

Chapter Ten

I'm a little early heading to the back to get changed for my set, but I want to give extra care to my appearance tonight. As I'm walking down the hallway I'm surprised to find Jager and Mike stepping out of an office I've never seen anyone in before.

"Have you made your decision yet?" I ask him with a teasing tone.

"I have. Would you join me to discuss it?"

Mike winks as he steps out of the door frame to allow me to enter.

"I only have a few minutes, I'm due on stage soon."

"That's all I need," he assures me, gesturing for me to enter the room ahead of him. Sighing, I precede him into the office as I try to pluck up that same courage I had earlier. The office is almost completely empty, just a massive wooden desk and a throne-like chair behind it. Not wanting to take the chair, I walk up to the desk and run my fingers along the surface, marveling at the stunning wood grain.

"Please, have a seat."

"Oh, I couldn't! That's obviously yours."

He closes the door on Mike's back and moves to take the massive chair. "Then sit with me."

Instead of sitting on his lap, I hop up to sit on the edge of the desk in front of him. "So, what have you decided?"

"As long as you don't fight me on other things, I won't fight you about not tipping."

"I can't promise you that! You seem to be a man who doesn't know how to restrain himself."

"I'm not. But that's the deal you have to make. Either you allow me to tip you and we have a purely professional relationship, or I'm not allowed to tip you and we can explore what's between us. I can be a patient man, Poppy, but I do take care of what's mine. If you decide you want to explore this, you'll be mine one hundred percent. Can you accept that? Because that means you'll have to accept some of those things that you think are too much."

Can I?

I examine him, trying to decide what it is I really want. I like working here and I love taking care of Gran, but since I had to quit school it feels like other than on stage and when I'm with him, nothing I'm doing is just for me anymore. There's no doubt I want this man, but can I keep up? He's older, richer, and seems far more powerful than I can probably even imagine.

But I do want him.

There's just one thing I need to know first, though, so I look down and take a bracing breath, my next words coming out more hesitantly than I intended. "Does that mean you'll be mine, too?"

"Absolutely."

I close my eyes, afraid of how that one word makes me feel, and finally give in to what I really want.

I nod.

"Tell me," he orders, lifting my chin with a single finger.

"Yes. Yes, I can accept that."

"Good girl," he praises me, then presses a soft kiss to my lips.

"Now go and dance, Sweet Poppy. And while you dance, know you have the undivided attention of everyone in that room, but mine is all that matters."

"Ruby," a man calls to me as I walk by. He tries to grab my arm but I see his hand coming and am able to maneuver away just in time to make him miss. "How much for a dance?"

Shoot! When I changed after my set I forgot I'd need to wear my waitress uniform so I wouldn't be asked to give dances! Is that even ok now? I turn to seek out Jager's attention, my eyes wide with panic, but all he does is tilt his head slightly and nod.

What the heck does that even mean?

"Yo!" the customer calls. "I asked, how much?"

Mike bends down to listen to what Jager has to say, then he starts making his way toward me.

"Hey, man!" the customer calls out when he reaches us. "I asked first!"

"Shut the fuck up," he snaps at the guy, then leans down to speak into my ear just loud enough that only I can hear him. "It's fine, Penelope. Jager wants you to give this guy a dance, but give him a show while you do it. Take that chair over there." He points to a chair a few yards away that's in Jager's direct line of sight. "Then head backstage." Straightening, he stares down the patron. "It's a hundred for the dance. Pay up."

The customer gulps but nods, pulling a bill out of his pocket and handing it to me.

"This way," I direct him, not taking his hand as I've seen other dancers do. I really don't want to touch this guy with Jager watching. Or really, at all. He's honestly kind of grubby looking. Mike simply winks at me and heads to the DJ booth, making a brief comment that I can only assume is a song request because he walks away just as quickly.

I step up to the side of the chair Mike directed me to and when I try to push it back so the man can sit, I realize it swivels. Smirking, I turn the chair so it faces Jager and allow the customer to sit. "Remember," I tell him, shaking a finger in his face, "no touching." He holds up his hands in surrender before gripping the end of the seat arms like he's supposed to, and the song that was playing fades out. "Sick Like Me" by In This Moment begins, and I circle him, dropping my head and letting my hair fall across my face to hide from view. I can still see everything through a small part in my curls, and that sliver lets me see that I have Jager's full attention. Ever so slowly, I smooth my hands down the back of the chair, giving the impression that I'm not quite sure what's coming, my body fluid and swaying slightly.

I watch Jager through the curtain of my hair, reveling in the fire I find in his eyes, then I fling my hair back out of my face and snap to attention when the drum beat hits. I lose myself in the song and the erratic strobe lights that are flashing to the beat throughout the club. I'm trying to bring out my inner goddess in hopes she can rival Maria Brink and refusing to lose eye contact with Jager until it's time to face my customer. Even then I guide him to turn the chair so while I straddle this unimportant man I can watch the only one who does matter watching me.

I'm already turned on by him just being in this room, but for some reason that I will need to examine later, using this faceless person to bring him any sort of pleasure is filling me with more lust than I've ever experienced! I can feel the arousal growing between my thighs, and there are multiple times I have to pretend I'm running my fingers over my pussy as a part of the dance, but it's really just to make sure that I'm not dripping through my panties and embarrassing myself.

When the song comes to a close I've somehow managed to bend myself over in a way that makes my customer believe the pose is for him, though it's really planned to show any potential wet spot to Jager. The moment the next song comes on it's like a switch flips and I realize what I've done. I straighten and snag the tip the customer is holding up for me and scurry to the back of the house as fast as I can without looking like I'm running to hide.

I've made it through the door and halfway down the hall when I hear a single word that stops me dead in my tracks.

"Poppy."

"Yes?" I ask without turning around to face him, worried I may have gone too far. I'd gotten so focused on my dance and the arousal running through me that I forgot to look at him when I'd finished. What if I went too far? If he's upset? I feel like I'm already in over my head and making mistakes. I've never known a man like him before and I don't know what the rules are!

"Come here."

Ok, so he doesn't sound mad. But he also sounds super quiet. Isn't that worse? Like a parent who isn't mad, just disappointed?

Wait, no. He's not anything like my parent. Gross.

I turn around without lifting my eyes from the floor and walk to him until I see his shoes.

"Did you enjoy that?" he asks me, voice still calm. I don't know how to answer. I did enjoy it, but now the worry is overtaking it. He said I was supposed to be his, then I go and give someone a lap dance? Isn't this why girls aren't supposed to bring boyfriends to their work? Or... wait. That was a movie and she was a singing bartender, not a stripper. But still. The point still stands, right?

Hands wrap around my waist and I'm turned and pressed up against the wall. I stare at his chest where I think I felt a nipple piercing before and pretend that if I don't look up he can't really be mad.

"Eyes up, little one," he orders. "Tell me."

Hesitating, I finally gather the courage to look up and meet his eyes. There's heat there, that's for sure.

But there's no anger.

"Wha– what was the question, again?"

"I want to know if dancing for another man while I watched turned you on."

"Oh," I whisper. "No."

"Are you sure?" he asks, hand skimming from my waist down to the edge of my panties and hooking underneath them to run his fingers up my slit, collecting the wetness that's gathered there. "Your wet pussy would say otherwise."

"I'm not lying!" I snap, finally feeling somewhat like myself again. He better not be calling me a liar!

"I'm not accusing you of lying, Poppy. But," he drawls, stroking my clit, "there is evidence to the contrary."

"It had nothing to do with the other man," I finally admit with a strained voice. "It's just because you were watching me."

He leans forward and dips his head so his lips are at my ear. "I could see it in your eyes, Sweet Poppy," he tells me while slowly slipping a finger inside me. "I could see it in your movements, and all I could think about was tasting you while you danced."

"Ta– tasting me?"

"Tasting you. Do you want that?"

"I..." My scrambled thoughts are interrupted by the sound of women's voices coming down the hall. I gasp, trying to remove his hands from my panties and failing when he simply holds me tighter.

"What's wrong, Sweetness?"

"People are coming!" I whisper shout.

"So?"

"We need to stop! They'll see!"

His silence as he continues stroking me almost convinces me it'll be ok if they see what he's doing to me, but I already have some trouble with my coworkers after my first night with that upset waitress and I don't want more. I frantically look around and notice I've been pressed up against the wall next to an office door. I don't know whose it is, but hopefully there's no one inside. I reach over and twist the knob, opening the door slightly and listening to see if anyone calls out.

Nothing.

I'm starting to feel the pleasure build and again consider staying put, but the voices are growing closer and I know I'll regret it later if I don't move now. I fling the door open and snag the center of Jager's shirt, dragging him along with me into the office and knowing all the way the only reason he came with me is because he allowed me to pull him. As soon as we're past the threshold he spins me and pins me aggressively against the wall once more.

"Please close the door," I whisper, looking up at him with pleading eyes. I'll dance for him in the center of the club all day, but I'm not ready for anyone to share these moments with us just yet.

Wait... yet?

My thoughts return to Jager as he grunts, leans over to grab the door handle, slams it shut and, showing he has my feelings in mind, flips the lock before dropping to his knees in front of me.

"Wha–?"

Suddenly I'm airborne. He's lifted me up and thrown me over his shoulder. He turns to walk toward the desk then pauses, grunting. Bracing my hands on his butt, I lift my head up as high as possible and try to look back over my shoulder.

"What's wrong?" I ask, trying to see what he's looking at.

"It seems our Trevor likes to watch."

"What do you mean?"

"He has cameras. Don't worry, I'll take care of it." He moves to the edge of the desk and lays me down gently, allowing me to see the massive TV setup Trevor has behind his desk. I gasp as I take in the cameras watching the most vulnerable areas of the club. The dance rooms, the stages, and even the locker room! Thank goodness I've never changed out in the main locker room area!

"Ignore it, Poppy," Jager instructs as he raises my skirt and removes my panties, lifting them to his nose and inhaling before stuffing them in his pants pocket. "Focus on me."

I do just that, forgetting about the screens and watching as he leans over me, draping his body over mine and licking up my neck before whispering directly into my ear.

"I know I'm the first to make you come, Little Poppy. But has anyone ever gotten you close by licking your pussy?"

"Um... no?"

"Are you not sure?" he asks, leaning back to meet my eyes.

"I'm sure. No one has ever done... that... before."

He jerks back in shock, examining my face as a slow, sensual grin forms on his beautiful lips.

"Brace yourself, Sweetness."

Pressing a kiss to my lips, he begins to nip, kiss, and lick his way down my body until he reaches my belly button. Instead of moving straight to my center, he presses a kiss there and backs up so he can kneel between my legs. Strong hands wrap around my hips and jerk me down onto a waiting tongue. I gasp and slap a hand over my mouth, not wanting to alert anyone of our presence in the office. Jager wastes no time being sweet or gentle; he sets upon me like a starving man — licking, sucking, and even biting me with a fervor that is honestly shocking. I can't help but release another gasp of pleasure when two fingers join his tongue, pumping in and out of me in time.

"Oh gosh," I pant, "oh goodness. Oh... oh..."

"Tell me," he says, having pulled away just long enough to get the words out before sucking my entire clit into his mouth and speeding up the motion of his fingers.

"Oh... *fuck*!" I whimper, unable to hold back as I feel myself rushing toward my second orgasm. My hand has somehow found his hair, and though I realize I probably shouldn't be gripping him like this I honestly can't control myself. I'm so close to coming I can barely breathe, and I'm almost there when the sound of the doorknob being jiggled reaches my ears and breaks through my haze of lust. I jerk into a sitting position when I hear Trevor's voice come muffled from the other side of the door.

"What the fuck? Who locked my door?"

"Shoot!" I snap quietly, pulling his hair and, unfortunately, his mouth off me. "Trevor is here!"

"So?"

Ugh! He needs to stop saying that!

"We need to stop!"

"Why?" he asks, standing and squinting at me suspiciously. I roll my eyes and accept his extended hand, hopping off the edge of the desk and making sure there's no mess left behind.

"Because it's... I don't want him to see me like this! He already looks at me too much, and I don't want him to see more of me. He gets enough when I'm on stage!" I whisper, getting angry as I point at the monitors all over the wall next to us. "What are we going to do?"

I look around frantically, finally realizing there's a second door to our left. Taking off at an almost run, I pull him toward the closet as I hear Trevor's key inserted into the lock. Thankfully it was already cracked open and the bi-fold door is relatively silent, so we sneak in and I'm able to close it as much as it was before Trevor opens the door.

"Who the fuck did that," he mutters to himself, ironically turning and locking the door behind him. He removes his tie as he walks over to the desk, and I cringe slightly as he walks past the corner where Jager just tasted me. If he only knew what happened there, he'd have a fit! Warmth surrounds me as Jager steps close and wraps his arms around me, nuzzling the hair on the top of my head as we both watch Trevor through the crack.

"Where the fuck is she?" Trevor curses, pulling up the cameras and searching through them to find someone.

"He's looking for you, Poppy," Jager whispers in my ear.

"Me?" I squeak, remembering to stay quiet at the last moment.

"Of course. Who else?"

"Gross," I lament.

"You don't like your admirer?" he asks, a hint of edge in his voice.

"No!" I scold him, turning around in his arms and making sure he can see my face in the limited light. "I never have. He's a nice guy, but I've never had feelings more than casual friendship for him. Barely even that."

"Well that's unfortunate," he responds, eyebrow raised.

"What? Why?" Does he not really want me? Or... wait. I narrow my eyes at him in anger. "I am not one of those girls you can just share around, mister!" I admonish. "Don't even think about it!"

Jager dips his head down until our noses are almost touching. "It's unfortunate for *him*. Turn around, sweet girl, and see what you do to him."

Turning as slowly as if I've just been told there's a killer behind me, when I see what he's referring to I almost wish I'd found a killer there instead.

There's a video of my most recent dance on all screens.

And he's masterbating.

Chapter Eleven

Seeing his penis in his hand is absolutely disgusting, and knowing he's touching himself and thinking of me? Nope! Not staying here for that! I begin to jerk away from Jager's hold so I can at least hide in the back of the closet without having to watch or hear him, but he holds me firmly in place.

"Don't even think about it," he purrs into my ear, melting me even in the face of what's going on in front of us. "There are two things going on in front of us right now. One is that your pathetic friend is touching himself while thinking of a woman he can and will never have." His hands finally leave my waist and migrate in opposite directions — one wrapping lightly around my throat and the other brushing my clit. "The other is on screen. The most stunning woman I've ever fucking seen is making a club full of people worship her. Most of them wish they could worship you like this, but they'll never have the chance."

His expert fingers are stoking the flames once more, and instead of watching Trevor touch himself, I simply close my eyes and lean my head back against his chest. "Worship me?" I ask, my hips beginning to roll to match his movements.

"If you haven't realized by now that I worship the ground you walk on, Sweet Poppy, you haven't been paying attention." My heart flutters as he places a delicate kiss on my temple, an act so in contrast with the way he's playing my body that it almost short circuits my mind. "Come for me, crimson goddess, then let me lay the world at your feet."

I can't help but obey, possibly climaxing more from his words then how he's playing my body.

By the time I calm enough to open my eyes and look up, I meet expectant eyes that are full of not only fire but also... tenderness? I can't figure out this man and why he'd possibly feel this way for me. A smile curves his lips and I see understanding there, but I don't want to ask what he's thinking and ruin the moment. Instead, I accept his offered kiss.

Because that's easier.

A clatter comes from the main office and Jager looks up, peering through the crack in the door and he stills.

"What?" I whisper, immediately concerned.

A rage filled gaze meets my own, and he jerks his gaze to the door, telling me without words to look for myself. I follow his gesture to find Trevor cleaning himself up. Gross. But that can't be what is making Jager so angry, can it? I look for what could possibly make him so immediately angry, but it takes me a few moments to understand what I'm seeing. When I do, I accidentally gasp so loud that Trevor actually hears me. He quickly hits a button on his keyboard before looking around at the main door to the office, probably worried he's about to get caught.

I'd be worried too, because he put cameras in Jager's office! I'm going to guess Jager didn't know or approve of it since his body is so stiff it feels like a hard hit could shatter him. Pulling his phone out, I watch as Jager texts Mike to get Trevor out of the office. I turn back to watch Trevor just as he hits another key and begins searching through the videos, mumbling to himself.

"Where is that fucker? I know he didn't leave. He won't leave Penny alone. Fucking asshole."

His constant mumbling and complaints are driving me crazy, so I finally breathe a sigh of relief when a booming knock sounds on the door.

"What?" he yells, turning off the monitors.

"Open up, asshole," Mike grumbles.

Trevor jumps up and adjusts his clothing, checking himself in the standing mirror to make sure he's all tucked back in, then rushes over to the door.

"What do you want, Mike? I'm busy."

"I want you to run this fucking club. There's been a fight up front. Jager may be taking care of pretty much everything these days, but I'm not your bitch, kid. Handle at least some of your shit."

"Fuck you, Mike! This is still my club." Trevor follows Mike out of the room and down the hall, and I can't help but giggle as I hear Mike's retreating voice land one last quip.

"Whatever you say, Chief."

Thankful that they're finally gone, I relax and lean back into Jager. "That was close."

"I wasn't concerned."

"Are you ever?" I ask, turning to face him and smiling.

"Not usually. Have dinner with me tomorrow."

He's not asking. He's not telling. He doesn't care that his change of topic didn't make my head spin.

He's simply stating it as if it's an inevitability.

I wish it were.

"I can't," I answer, my disappointment lifting when I notice what would be a pout on anyone other than him. Ok so it's definitely a pout.

"Why not." Again, not a question

"I promised Gran we'd spend the day together. She has treatment and she hasn't been doing very well after. I want to stay with her to make sure she's ok and try to make her something to eat that she can keep down."

"Are the meals I've been sending not helping? I can get another chef."

"No! They definitely are, and I can never thank you enough. I just want to make her a family recipe. It's her great grandmother's stew, we always make it when someone is sick." I shrug sheepishly and wince a little as I pluck up the courage to ask my next question. I feel a little silly, like it'll prove our age difference, but I want to build something with this man. Our relationship can't all be strip clubs and fancy dinners — that's just not reality. "Maybe... maybe you could come over after she's gone to bed? She goes down pretty early after treatment. We could watch a movie or something."

"Watch... a movie?" he asks, brow furrowed. "Is that the 'Netflix and chill' thing I've heard about?"

"No," I laugh. "I mean it. Watch. A. Movie."

He sighs, then looks me up and down, considering. "Will there be stew?"

My heart flutters for a moment, the idea of feeding him and relaxing together after a long day lighting something inside me that I never expected. Yes, I did tell him I'd give him my everything, but I think there was a part of me that never imagined he'd want something more than just a purely physical, surface-level relationship.

It suddenly hits me how desperately I want this. I want this man, and I want to build a life with him.

"And bread."

"Bread?"

"Homemade," I nod.

"Consider it done. Just tell me what time to be there."

"I'll text you, it'll be after eight." I stand up on my toes, stretching to give him a kiss on the lips, then wave as I head down the hall to the changing rooms. I need to clean up and get back on the floor for the last portion of my shift.

"Hey, Sugar!" Mina quips as I pass her office. "Good night so far?"

"Great," I respond, grinning and wiggling my eyebrows. Other than Jager and the confidence I have found with dancing for the patrons, Mina is my favorite part of my new job.

"What are you doing tomorrow night? Any fun plans? Are you going to go out on the town? You've been on for six days straight, you deserve a break!"

"Girl, you ain't lying!" I laugh. "I actually promised Gran I'd stay home with her, so it'll just be us relaxing. She has treatment tomorrow and she's feeling pretty rough after each session these days."

"Oh honey, I'm so sorry. Is she doing ok in general?"

"I guess. She doesn't rea–"

"Mina!" Trevor snaps, turning the corner and not caring that he's interrupting our conversation. "We had a fight. Add these guys to the banned list, now!"

"Trevor!" I scold, not liking how he talks to my friend.

"What?"

"Stop being so rude. She's an employee of the club, not a slave."

His shoulders droop, and he runs a hand through his hair. "Sorry Penny-" at the sight of my narrowed eyes, he finishes my name like I continually ask him to. "-elope."

I raise an eyebrow and jerk my head toward Mina, who is standing across from me with wide eyes.

"Sorry, Mina," he apologizes reluctantly. "It's been a rough night."

"No worries. I'll add them." She takes the paperwork and ignores Trevor from that moment on, calling to me over her shoulder as she walks into her office.

"Have a good night with Gran tomorrow, Sugar. Get some rest. You deserve the night off!"

Chapter Twelve

Gran is thankfully, finally asleep. Treatment today was rough, and she couldn't keep the stew down when she tried to eat dinner. She went to bed earlier than I had anticipated, and I sat with her until she was finally sound asleep after tossing and turning for about an hour. I texted Jager to let him know he could come over early, but he was stuck in a meeting he had scheduled specifically for when I'd be unavailable and had to finish up before heading over.

Happy to have a little time to myself to relax after such a stressful day, I checked the stew to make sure it was still warm and ready for him and hopped in the shower to decompress. My first instinct was to put on makeup and style my hair, but decided against it. He'll see me like this at some point if we continue seeing each other, so it might as well be sooner rather than later. I hear the distant roll of thunder as I apply my face lotion, and I smile knowing that this will be the perfect night to snuggle up with a scary movie. He won't be here for another two hours, so I decide to get started without him and turn on my comfort movie — *Saw*.

The original; not those ridiculous sequels.

I've never found a movie that has genuinely scared me, but if anything has come close it's this one — specifically the scene where a man crawls out the back of the car wearing the pig mask.

Five minutes into the movie, I get a text.

Jager

This meeting is boring as fuck. What are you doing?

I can't help but giggle at the idea of Jager texting me to complain in the middle of a meeting that was so important he had to finish it before coming over.

> Well finish up so you can get here! Your dinner is ready and I just started a movie.

> You're really going to feed me?

> Of course I am! I may have also made dessert.

> You ARE dessert.

> Fine. I'll finish up here and be there as soon as possible.

> See you soon ;)

Ironically, just as the strobe starts flashing on the pig-man, lightning strikes right outside the house and illuminates what I am sure is the figure of a man looking in my living room window. He quickly jumps and runs out of sight, but I am certain that whoever he is was looking in the window and not just passing by.

> Jager, I'm scared.

> I think someone was just looking in my window!

Instead of the expected text response, my phone immediately rings.

"Poppy, I need you to smile like you're happy to hear from me, can you do that?"

I clear my throat and force the most natural smile I can manage onto my face — pretty sure I'm failing. "I can definitely try."

"Good girl. I need you to act completely natural for me. I have some men en route and I'm on my way to you. What are the chances that someone was just walking by?"

"Um... none? It's my backyard, and it's fenced, so regardless it's someone who shouldn't be there."

"Ok. They're five minutes from your location. What is a room that is relatively close and safe for you to go to?"

"The... the laundry room. It's off the kitchen."

At this point I'm so afraid I can't keep a smile on my face, so I've just buried my head in my knees in case the person looks in the window again. That looks natural... right?

"Good. I want you to get up and go check on the food. Act as calm as you can, then go into the laundry room and wait. Can you get to a knife while you're checking on the food?"

"Yes," I answer in a small voice, taking a deep breath and getting up to do as he says. The kitchen is behind the living room, and luckily the bread is on a cooling rack next to the stove, directly next to the knife block.

"Keep talking to me, Sweetness. Let me know you're ok. I'm on my way. I promise nothing will happen to you." His reassuring words provide a modicum of reassurance, but comforting words do not change the fact that I'm in this house, basically alone, with someone uninvited creeping in my backyard. Maybe I'm freaking out over nothing. Perhaps it was just my imagination. Was it even real?

"Do you think this is necessary? I was watching a scary movie. Maybe I imagined it? I don't want to put you or your men out. Maybe I shouldn't have sent you that text. I'm tired. I definitely probably imagined it."

"I don't care if you imagined it or not, I expect you to call me when something like this happens. I'm going to take care of you, regardless. My men are three minutes away."

"Ok."

I lift the lid off the stew pot and inhale deeply, hoping the rich scent will help me relax. It doesn't, but seeing the double batch I made in hopes that Jager would like it and want to take some home calms me, slightly.

He's coming for me.

For the first time in my life, I have someone who cares enough to drop what he's doing and rush to my side. Someone other than Gran who truly wants to take care of me.

My mom couldn't even care enough to try.

I pick up the largest knife I have and slice the end off the fresh loaf, taking a bite to seem more normal. I held off on eating when Gran couldn't so I could share the meal with Jager, so even though I am scared, I'm hungry. "Ok, I have a knife and I'm going to the lau–" I stop mid sentence, terrified at the sound now coming from the door.

"Poppy?"

His voice is harsh, demanding an answer to why I've stopped speaking so abruptly.

"Jager," I whisper. "I think someone's trying to get in! They're messing with the door knob!"

"Fuck! Which door? They're almost there, get into the laundry room, now!"

I scurry into the laundry room, still clutching the knife and more scared than I've ever been. "The back door, off the kitchen. It's deadbolted but it sounds like they're trying to pick it!"

"They're one minute out, just hold on for me."

"I'm scared, Jager."

"I know, baby. We're almost there."

Thunder crashes so loud above that I jump and scream, but it's followed by the sound of shouting — the intruder has been caught off guard by the arrival of Jager's men.

"They're here! I think they're chasing him!"

"Good. Just stay where you are until I arrive, I'm less than three minutes away."

"Ok."

Jager spends the next two and a half minutes consoling me and giving me a play by play of what's happening as it's being relayed to his driver, and when he tells me he's arrived and is at my front door, I drop the knife and run to let him in. Throwing the door open, I'm met with the sight of the most beautiful man I've ever seen, dripping wet from rain and full of both softness and rage. My phone falls from my fingers and clatters to the floor as I jump into his arms, wrapping my entire body around him and burying my face in his neck as I begin to sob.

What if they'd come in and hurt Gran? Hurt me? She doesn't have anyone else to care for her, and I couldn't live with her being taken from me like that.

"Shhh, it's ok, Sweetness. I've got you now. I'm here." I can feel myself being carried through the house after the door is closed and locked quietly behind him. He takes a seat in the living room and whispers sweet words meant to calm and reassure me, and by the time a quiet knock sounds on the front door, I've at least calmed enough to climb off him so he can answer it.

Mike is there, soaking wet and pissed. I jump up and run to the laundry room to grab both of them clean towels, allowing the men to discuss whatever happened without me. He'll tell me what I need to know. Probably. Do I even want to know details?

"I'm sorry, Penelope," Mike laments. "He got away. Fuck!" he curses, shaking his head and staring up at the ceiling.

"Are you sure there was someone there? I didn't just imagine it?" I ask, hoping for something I know isn't possible while handing first Jager, then Mike, a towel.

"There was definitely someone there," Jager tells me, using the towel to attempt to dry his hair. His clothes are soaked through! I should have thought about that before climbing him like a mentally unstable spider monkey. "There are shoe impressions outside the living room window and scratch marks on the back door locks. Do you have any idea who it could have been?"

"No, but I'm sure you can tell this isn't the best neighborhood. Gran and I haven't ever had any problems, but maybe it was just our turn?"

"Maybe," Mike muses, thanking me for the towel as he hands it back. He's still dripping wet, but at least his face and hair are relatively dry. "We're going to keep searching the area and post up outside to make sure they don't come back."

I look at Jager and his expression dares me to argue, so I just leave it. "Ok. Thank you both for coming so quickly. I..."

"I know," Jager says, kissing the top of my head.

"Mike, are you staying?" I ask.

"No, thanks though. I'm going to see what I can figure out outside."

"But it's storming!"

"Exactly. If it keeps going we may lose evidence."

Fair enough, I guess.

"Are you staying? I ask Jager, worried he wants to search the premises with Mike.

"Of course I am. I was promised dinner."

"Damnit, I knew I should have said yes," Mike grumbles, then winks at me when Jager growls menacingly. "Kidding, boss!" he says, hands up in surrender. "I'll call you when I know something."

"Good."

Mike turns to exit the house but I tell him to wait, then rush off to the coat closet. We didn't keep much of my Pop's stuff, but we did keep his old raincoat for emergencies. It swallows Gran and me like a dress, but it should fit Mike.

"Here, this should fit you."

"Whose is that?" Jager grumbles.

"It was my grandfather's, silly. Mike, I want you to at least stay somewhat dry if you're out there because of me."

"Thanks, Penelope."

"You can call me Pen," I tell him, blushing slightly under their surprised scrutiny. "What? I may not like Penny, but Penelope is a mouthful."

Jager's scowl turns into a wicked smile. "A delicious mouthful."

"And on that note, I'm out of here. Night, boss. Night, *Pen*."

"Goodnight. Please stay safe! Mina would kill me if you got hurt!"

"You got it, Boss Number Two!" He smiles, salutes, and heads back into the rain.

I lock the door behind him, then turn to Jager, hands on hips. "Now, let's get you cleaned up."

"What do you mean?" he asks, looking down at his clothes. He's not messy, just wet.

"Come on," I tell him, taking his hand and pulling him into the kitchen with me. "Let me get you some dinner, then I'll get you some dry clothes."

"I don't think we're the same size," he quips, possibly making the first true joke I've heard since we met.

"Funny guy!" I chuckle, ladling the piping hot stew into a large bowl and cutting off a chunk of fresh bread. I direct him to take a seat at the table and place it all in front of him, along with a beer. "Can I get you anything else?"

Before I can blink I'm in his lap, returning a kiss that's so passionate I feel like my panties are going to melt off. Jager pulls back from me and cups my face with both hands.

"I thought I was going to lose you. I just found you, Poppy. Don't scare me like that again."

"I didn't mean to!" I argue quietly, trying to keep my heart from fluttering out of my chest. My voice becomes smaller as I admit my own fears. "I was so scared,

Jager. I was afraid you wouldn't be able to get here in time. I was afraid you'd get hurt if you did."

"I will always get here in time, I promise. No one is taking you away from me. You promised me everything, and I always collect."

I press a sweet kiss to his lips and smile when he wipes an errant tear from my cheek with his thumb. I don't typically cry this much. Is this what it feels like to let yourself be vulnerable for once? On one hand, I love being able to let go. On the other, as Gran would say, "Momma didn't raise no bitch."

"Ok," I say, pulling all of my strength together to keep myself from telling this man I'm falling for him. "Let me get you some dry clothes. Go ahead and eat."

He nods and allows me to stand, watching as I leave the room and head down the hall toward Gran's room. I sneak in, worried about waking her. She's sleeping, but fitfully, and it kills me to see the pain and discomfort she's in, but I'm so thankful she slept through everything that happened. Wetting a washcloth in her bathroom, I ring it out and fold it to place on her forehead, hoping that will help make her a bit more comfortable. I find my Pop's old sweats folded in the back of her closet exactly where I expected, and lift them to my nose to inhale his old pipe tobacco scent. It's been years since he passed, but somehow the smell lingers with some of his things, no matter how many times they're washed or cleaned. It instantly calms my racing heart.

Jager is still sitting at the kitchen counter where I left him, but the sight stops me when I enter. He hasn't touched his food, and there's a second bowl on the table next to him, filled to the brim. The cutting board with bread is beside it, the bread now sliced halfway. There's also a glass of tea.

Who is this man?

"I... Thank you. You didn't have to do that."

"You promised me dinner. I want to eat it with you."

I blush, then awkwardly hold out the sweats. "I know they're not exactly your style, but this is all we have that will fit you. If you want to change, I can hang up your clothes to dry."

"Thank you," he says, taking them and bending to kiss me. "Where?"

"You can change in my room." I direct him to follow me down the hall, then quietly let him inside. We're thankfully separated from Gran's room by my bathroom, so our conversation shouldn't wake her.

A lot of my childhood memorabilia is still displayed on the walls and dresser, and I sit on my bed while he takes it all in.

"Who is this?" he asks, holding out a framed picture of me with my mother when I was a toddler.

"Oh, that's me and my mom."

"She looks young to be a mother," he muses. "Where is she now?"

"She died. Not too long after that photo was taken, actually."

He places the photo back down on the shelf and moves to sit next to me. "How? If you don't mind me asking."

"No, it's ok. She was fifteen when she had me, which is why Gran is such a young grandmother. Mom was in a car accident not long after I was born and got addicted to pain pills." My voice has taken on the matter-of-fact tone it always does when I tell this story. "She moved from pills to harder drugs and eventually bought from the wrong dealer. She took something laced with fentanyl and died right before my third birthday."

"I'm so sorry, Penelope. Where is your father?"

"We don't know. Mom either didn't know who he was or didn't want to say. My grandparents officially took me in after Mom died, though they'd basically already been raising me. Pop died when I was eleven. It's been me and Gran against the world ever since."

"Not anymore," he tells me, taking my chin and forcing me to meet his eyes. "It'll never be just the two of you again."

Tears come unbidden again, surprising me with the absolute devastation that one statement fills me with. It's been just us for so long. We've struggled. We've had really hard times, but we've always made it through, together. I'm tired of struggling, though, and the idea that this man wants to lighten my load and walk beside me is almost more than I can handle.

Instead of responding, I simply raise up on my knees, wrap my arms around his neck, and kiss him. He's usually the one to initiate physical contact, and I want to show him that I want and need him as much as he seems to want and need me. I suck in a breath at the cold sensation of his wet clothes against my breasts, so I pull back and begin to unbutton his shirt. He allows me to, and tight, tanned skin is revealed with each freed button. Halfway down his chest I remember something and pull the gaping shirt aside. I was right! He does have a nipple piercing. Gosh, that's sexy.

Wait... you know what? No more gosh. No more shoot or darn.

That's *fucking* sexy.

I'm a grown ass woman who is empowered enough to strip in front of strangers and take off this grown ass man's shirt. I can be adult enough to say things like fuck.

Especially since I think I'm finally about to do just that.

Chapter Thirteen

I pull back and meet his eyes, trying to figure out the question that meets me there.

"What?" I ask, not sure if something is wrong.

"Tell me."

"Tell you what?"

"Tell me what you want, sweet girl."

I shrug, trying to hide my nervousness but unable to hold back a blush. "I just want you."

I lean back and lift my shirt over my head, dropping it to the floor. I take my clothes off in front of strangers for a living, now. I've had this man's face buried between my thighs. For some reason, though, sitting in my childhood bedroom and taking my clothes off for him makes me feel more vulnerable than anything ever has.

"You're beautiful," he tells me quietly, leaning back on his hands and allowing me to take the lead for once. I stand in front of him and unhook my bra, allowing the straps to fall from my shoulders before I drop it carelessly to the floor. Surprisingly, his eyes never leave mine. Hooking my thumbs in the sides of my shorts and panties I drop those as well, then step out of them before dropping to my knees directly in front of him. I spread his legs wide enough to allow me to kneel between them and return to unbuttoning his shirt. My hands reach his belt buckle and I finally look back up at him, my lip pinched so hard between my teeth I'm worried it may start bleeding.

"Show me what you want, Poppy, or we can stop right now. Tonight was scary for you, we can go eat dinner and relax while you recover."

I pause and think about it for the briefest second before realizing I have no intention of stopping.

I release my lip and lick away the sting, then unbuckle his belt and immediately free him from his pants. He's huge. For a moment I worry that I won't be able to fit him in my mouth, but no matter what, I'm going to try my best.

"Will you tell me if I do it wrong?"

Heavy lidded eyes crinkle in the corners and a thumb slides in between my lips. I lick the pad before sucking it gently deeper into my mouth. "Trust me," he purrs. "You'll do just fine."

I begin sucking on his thumb as if it was my ultimate goal and wrap my fingers around his hard length, matching the rhythm of both to elicit a grunt from him that makes me smile. Jager removes his thumb and instead threads his fingers through my hair, pulling me forward and searing me with a kiss that literally curls my toes and instinctively tightens my grip around him. I want to get lost in his kiss, but I also don't want to be distracted anymore, so I pull back and *tell him:*

"I'm going to suck your cock now."

His shocked blink is exactly the reaction I was going for, and I drop to lick him from base to tip. His hips flex slightly, arching toward me and showing me how much he liked that, so I continue to do it for a few moments, licking him like he's the sweetest ice cream, dripping on a hot summer day. His fingers tighten in my hair for a fraction of a second before releasing me completely, but my hand snaps up and directs him to replace it.

He likes being in control. I don't want that to stop now.

I finally take his tip into my mouth, stretching almost to the point of pain, but I'm determined to make him feel as good as he's made me. I take him into my mouth as far as possible before it gets uncomfortable, and I'm disappointed to realize there's so much length left! I've heard about deep throating, but I don't think that's possible with him. Maybe I'll be able to do it with practice? All I know is I won't be able to do it tonight, so I wrap a hand around his base and slide it up and down to meet my mouth with each stroke, trying to get deeper every time. Jager's grip on my hair tightens slowly, but it's still not tight enough. I reach up with my free hand and direct him to tighten it even further and place pressure on him to try to indicate I want him to direct my tempo.

He gets the message.

His grip tightens and he begins using it as leverage to control my depth and pace. At first it's difficult to keep up, and I get embarrassed because drool is starting to slip out of my mouth. He groans once it reaches my hand and lubricates my movements, and I realize the drooling is a positive thing, so I let it happen. He's firm and demanding, but he's also careful. Careful not to grip my hair too tight or push me too far down on his cock that I choke. I realize if I just allow him to control my movements and relax my mouth and throat, I can go deeper, so I do just that.

"Fuck," he murmurs. "You look so fucking sexy with my cock buried in your mouth. Can you take more of me, Sweet Poppy?"

I don't know if I can, but I'm willing to try. I lift my eyes to his, unable to speak with a dick in my mouth. I nod.

"Good girl," he coos, running the fingers of his other hand through my hair so he's holding my head on both sides. Slowly, he begins pushing me further down his length while also arching his hips upward. It's further than I've gone before, and my mouth is starting to get sore, but I also want to please him. He finally hits the back of my throat and my gag reflex is triggered, causing a completely embarrassing gawking sound.

"Such a good girl." He finally pulls me completely off him and uses his grip on my hair to straighten me so I'm once again kneeling tall. "Time to get on the bed, little one. On your knees, hold the headboard." I'm so dazed from the high of being called a good girl while his cock was in my mouth, it takes me a second to comply. Once I'm in place I look back at him but he simply clucks his tongue at me. "Face the wall, Penelope."

Ok, so I love it when he calls me Poppy. Or Sweetness. Or even, baby. But Penelope? In that deep, aroused voice?

I may have just come without him even touching me.

Fabric rustles behind me and then the bed shifts. I squeal when fingers wrap around my waist and yank me down onto his waiting mouth. Terrified I'll suffocate him I try to lean forward to take the pressure off him, but he simply growls and won't let me move.

He was somewhat delicate when he went down on me at the club, but he's almost like a man possessed as he licks me now. His tongue splits my lower lips and he sucks my clit into his mouth almost immediately, then he moves lower and spears his tongue inside me. I have to slap a hand over my mouth as a loud, long groan falls from me. I cannot imagine what would happen if Gran walked in here right now!

I lean forward slightly, unable to stop myself from grinding down on his face, and though I'm concerned about his potential lack of oxygen, I remind myself he put himself in this situation.

If he dies, he dies.

His growl vibrates against my skin and it distracts me so well I don't realize he's slipped his fingers inside until he begins pumping them in and out of me.

"Oh, fuck," I groan. He just chuckles and doubles his efforts, pushing me faster toward my climax. Mere seconds before I come, I bury my face in a pillow as I scream out my release, desperately grinding down onto his face and fingers.

I thought I'd come before? I'm pretty sure whoever it was that called an orgasm a "little death" is spot on, because my life just flashed before my eyes.

Jager continues licking me until my movements slow. Eventually, it almost becomes too much and I beg him to let me go so I can catch my breath. He finally places a sweet kiss to my clit, then releases me so I can fall to the side. He snags a tissue from the box next to my bed and wipes his mouth before kissing me, then pulls me to him so he's leaning over me.

"You are a goddess," he tells me, lightly skimming his hands over my body. "Do you know that?"

"No," I giggle between pants of air. "Pretty sure goddesses would have more stamina than me."

"Does that mean we're done for the evening?" he asks, his face not giving away what he's thinking.

"No!" I insist, then catch myself. "I mean, unless you are."

"I could never get enough of you," he tells me. His face is completely calm and earnest, so I really do think he means it. "But this is completely up to you. Our dinner is getting cold."

I simply nod, waiting to hear those two words that are starting to be all it takes to move me.

"Tell me."

There they are!

Am I supposed to tell him I'm a virgin? Does that even matter? I don't want him to think less of me, but he probably already assumes so since I've never even performed oral sex before. Or had an orgasm before.

Screw it, I'm not going to make things weird. I'm sure he knows. Right?

"I'm on birth control."

That gets me an eyebrow raise, then the sexiest smirk I've ever seen.

"Good girl," he whispers, dipping his head and taking my nipple in his mouth. "Tell me," he breathes against my skin. "Tell me what you want."

"I want…" I clear my throat, trying to make him feel like his words make me feel. "No. I need you inside me," I admit. "Please, Jager."

He stills at my admission, then shifts so he's over top of me and wraps my legs around him.

"Are you sure?" he asks, taking his dick in hand and stroking it slowly as he watches me for any signs of hesitation.

"I'm sure. Please."

He looks down only long enough to direct the head of his cock to my opening, then meets my eyes once more, watching me as he slowly pushes his way inside.

I heard that it could be uncomfortable the first time, but this hurts! I try to keep the pain from my face, but he must be able to tell because he stops all forward movement.

"Are you ok?" he asks, concern lining his voice.

"Yeah… um. It's just… a lot of pressure." I try to downplay the discomfort I'm in but he's not buying it. He tries to pull back out but I grab him and pull him toward me. "I'm ok! It's just more than I thought it would be. Please, don't stop."

"Are you sure?"

"Yes," I tell him, certain. "I want this."

He watches me for a moment before beginning to move slowly again. Each movement is only slightly faster and deeper, as if he's more concerned about my comfort than his pleasure. The discomfort starts to fade slowly, and I begin rocking my hips in time with his.

Jager leans back slightly, putting just enough space between us to help facilitate his next request. "Touch yourself for me," he says, eyes fixed on where he's sliding in and out of me. I move one hand down and begin to stroke my clit in time with his movements, and the added stimulation decreases the ache even further. "Spread yourself with your other hand, Sweetness. Let me see."

My other hand moves to obey him before I even realize what I'm doing, and once I'm spread wide and touching myself while he slowly works his cock in and out of me I feel an orgasm begin to build again.

"That's it, let yourself go. Come for me again, little one."

My fingers speed up of their own volition and he increases his thrusts to match my pace, still being careful to not go too deep. My toes begin to curl and my body tightens up, and the moment my orgasm crashes over me he slams his lips to mine, and his cock completely home. He devours my kiss and my scream, one of both pleasure and pain, and lets me ride out the tide at my own pace. Once my scream dies his own head is thrown back and his pace stutters just slightly as he releases a long, drawn out, "Fuck."

He pulses inside me, then droops as if he's just lost most of his energy, gently pulling out of me and rolling over to the side so he doesn't crush me. I look down, reveling in what we just shared, and gasp in horror. His dick has blood on it!

I knew that was a possibility, but didn't really think it would really happen.

"Oh my God! I'm so sorry! Oh shoot!" Old habits apparently die hard. I try to jump up from the bed but he simply holds me to him.

"What's wrong?" he asks, confusion lining his face. "Are you ok?"

"You–, I–"

I don't even know what to say so I just gesture at his crotch frantically. "I'm so sorry!"

He finally looks to where I'm pointing and smiles serenely, leaning back against my pillows and tucking his hands behind his head.

"There's nothing to be sorry about, Penelope. I asked you to give me everything, and this is a huge part of that." My cheeks heat at the affection in his voice, and I finally calm down.

"Can I, I don't know, at least get you a towel or something to clean up?"

"No," he growls, pulling me to him and cradling me at his side. "After that gift? You're not leaving my side."

Chapter Fourteen

"Penelope Channing, who are all of these men?"

I jump at the sound of Gran's voice scolding me from the hallway, wincing slightly as it creates a stinging reminder of what we did together last night. On the positive side, she's got enough energy and is feeling well enough to bring out the angry voice, but I guess that's also a negative for me right now.

"Oh, um…"

"Ms. Channing?" Jager asks, standing from the kitchen table and buttoning his suit jacket as he stands.

"Yes? Who the fuck are you?"

"Gosh, Gran! Be nice!"

"Why? Who is he?"

Before Jager can answer, I step in front of him and take over. "Gran, this is Mr. Conri."

"Your boss?"

"Um… sort of?"

"No ma'am," he interrupts, stepping up beside me and placing a hand on my hip. "I'm an investor in the club where she works, but I'm in no way her superior."

My eyes pop wide at the double meaning he's putting out there, and Gran's narrow at the sight of the hand on my waist.

"So now that I know who you are, why are you here? And who are all these other brutes?"

"These are my men, and they are here your protection."

"Whose protection?" she asks, suspicious.

"Gran, we had a prowler last night. I called Jager and he sent his men over to check things out until he could get here."

"Did you call the police?"

"No, ma'am. The men are former officers and can handle the situation more appropriately than the police. Not as many restrictions."

"Gran, why don't you sit down and we'll explain everything."

"Screw that. Move over. If they're here they're getting breakfast."

Jager initially wasn't too happy about us inviting his men to eat with us, but Gran wouldn't hear anything to the contrary. They risked themselves all night watching the house for us; the least we could do was feed them.

I'm glad she initiated that argument, because it meant I didn't have to.

Surprisingly, his men insisted on washing the dishes and cleaning up while Gran, Jager, and I took our coffee to the living room so they could chat more. Eventually, a knock sounds at the front door and Jager rises from his spot next to me on the couch, directing Gran and me to stay seated.

"Is it Mike?" I ask, not sure who else would be here at this time of the morning.

"No." No answer as to who it is, just, "no."

He answers the door and shakes the hand of the man standing in front of three others. "Thanks for coming," he tells him, stepping back and letting them in. "I want the full package, including the night vision and infrared. Visible and hidden. Inside and out, and I want it done today."

"Excuse me," I say, expecting him to give me his full attention. When he doesn't, I stand and walk toward him. "Jager!"

All four of the new arrivals are staring at me with mouths dropped practically to the floor, but I don't care.

"Yes, Sweetness?"

"Don't give me that shit! Who are they and what is this? What is the full package? Infrared? Night vision? Hidden?"

"Robert and his crew are my security team. They're here to install a new system for you."

"But I don't want–"

"Poppy, I know what you're thinking, but you agreed to this. I can't change who I am."

"Penny, what is he talking about?"

"Ms. Channing, I understand what this looks like," he tells her, "but when your granddaughter agreed to see me I explained that I can be overbearing at times. I protect who and what are important to me. She very much falls under my protection, and as her grandmother, my protection extends to you as well."

My heart flutters with his honestly, and I can see it affecting Gran as well.

"Can we discuss it?" she asks, head tilted in thought.

"We can discuss whatever you'd like, but the security system will still be installed today, exactly to my specifications and requirements. For the safety of both of you. I don't want anything to happen to her, and I know it would devastate her if something happened to you."

Gran huffs, leans back against the couch with her arms crossed, and assesses the man who maybe just almost said he loved me. She looks at me, then nods.

"Go ahead."

"Gran!"

"No, Penny. He's right. If we did have a prowler, we may not be safe. I'd rather be safe than sorry."

"Look at it this way," he says, turning back to face me and angling my face to his. "It's either this, or you both move into my place. Your choice."

"Fine!" I growl. "But I'm not going to be happy about it!"

"Understood." He turns to the waiting men and simply nods and jerks his chin toward the back of the house for them to get to work.

"Additionally, if I may be so bold, Ms. Channing?"

"Yes?"

"I won't ask Penelope to stop working and allow me to help you financially, because she won't appreciate tha–"

"Hell no I wouldn't!"

"–and, I know she enjoys working," he finishes, turning to me, unimpressed by my interruption. "That being said, would you permit me to arrange a nurse to attend you on the nights she works?"

"What?" I ask, shocked. "Why?"

"Because you worry about her," he shrugs.

"That's very generous, Mr. Conri," Gran starts, but he corrects her.

"Jager, please."

"Jager. But that's too much. I couldn't accept."

"Please," he says, a word I don't think I've ever heard him say. "If not for your own sake, for hers. She really does worry."

"You do?" Gran asks, leaning forward and scrutinizing my face.

"Of course I do! What if you start to feel worse and I'm not here to help? I want you to be safe and healthy, but I also have to work. I'd have asked you to let me hire one, but you would never let me."

"Did you ask him to do this, then?"

"No! No, Gran, I promise this was completely his idea. We've never even discussed it."

Gran closes her eyes and sighs, knowing she's been defeated.

"Fine. I'll allow it. But only on nights when I'm not feeling well!"

"I'll take it!" I squeal, hugging her quickly before she huffs her way out of the room, then running back to Jager and jumping into his arms. "Thank you." My whisper is heartfelt, and the smile it earns me is reflected warmly in his eyes.

I'm falling so hard for this man.

"Penelope?" Gran calls, voice an obvious mix of irritation and confusion.

"Yes?" I answer between pressing kisses to Jager's face.

"I'm going to start a load of delicates."

"Ok!"

"Just one question," she continues.

I sigh. "Yes?"

"Why did someone stab my floor?"

Oops.

JAGER

"We need to talk, Conri."

I don't look up from the paperwork on my desk, but I can sense that it's both Felix and Trevor in my office now. "I'm busy."

"Fuck that! You're always busy. This is important!"

What could either of these men possibly have to say that's important to me?

"What is it, Felix? You have two minutes."

"Someone is taking money from the club."

"How much?" Let's see if they've been smart enough to figure out exactly what's going on.

"Thousands per night!" Trevor interjects.

I finally set my pen down and look up at them, leaning back in my chair and crossing my arms over my chest.

"For how long?"

"At least a week," he admits, chest puffed out like he deserves a fucking cookie for getting the answer wrong.

"Only that long?" I ask, cocking my head to the side and showing him I'm unimpressed.

"I said at least. We came to you as soon as we figured out that it was happening."

"Then you came too soon," I tell him, playing with him like a cat does with a mouse. "Though I'd wager coming too soon is something you're familiar with. Regardless, you're late to the game."

"What the fuck does that even mean? We came to you with the problem as soon as we knew it existed!"

"You came to me with yet another problem you expected me to fix, without the answers you should have known I would want. You came to me with *yet another problem* that you're unable to determine the severity of or solve without my help."

"Listen–" Felix starts.

"You came to me with a problem that isn't mine, but yours."

"What the fuck are you talking about, Conri? This is your problem too because you're an investor!"

"First, it's been happening for over a month, not at least a week."

"What?" Felix yelps, turning to Trevor with murder in his eyes.

"Second," I interrupt, "No one is stealing from the club. I'm simply taking what I'm owed."

"What do you mean?" Trevor asks, shrinking before us as Felix glares at him.

"I mean just what I said. I've been taking a cut every night for the past six weeks. Not only is it my money and investment I'm protecting and recouping, but it proves to me that you two are exactly the businessmen I believed you to be. If it took you six weeks to realize you're sixty thousand dollars down, it's no wonder your businesses are failing."

"What the fuck, Conri!" Felix shouts, storming forward to the edge of my desk, his oily face turning beet red. "That was not our agreement!"

"I rewrote it."

Instead of arguing further, Felix picks up the crystal paperweight Penelope gave me last week as an "Office Warming" gift and throws it across the room, causing it to shatter against the brick wall on impact.

Big mistake.

I stand slowly, causing both of them to stiffen as if I'm about to start slicing them, but that's not going to happen tonight. My girl goes on stage shortly and I don't want her distracted when she sees blood on my clothes. I step around the desk and make my way to Trevor. Instead of making any statement, I slam my first into his gut so hard the wind is knocked out of him and he drops to his knees, curling in on himself as he tries to breathe.

"Knock, knock!" Penelope's voice calls from the opening door. "Oh gosh, what happened?"

Obviously surprised, she hurries toward us, extending her hand down to Trevor's prone form, then pausing her movement almost as quickly. She looks at me as if worried I'll be upset with her for helping him. She's not wrong. Normally, if I put someone on the ground I wouldn't be ok with her helping them, but she can't help herself. That's just who she is. She's known him for many years, and she always wants to help when she sees someone hurting. I simply nod and press a quick kiss to her temple, then return to my desk to finish my paperwork.

I'd asked her to let me know when she arrived for the evening so I could head to my table. I didn't anticipate the dumbass duo interrupting my stolen moments with her, and I'm not happy.

"I'm fine!" Trevor snarls, obviously embarrassed and jerking away from her offered hand. He scrambles to feet, attempting to act as if he wasn't just dropped without a thought.

"Oh, ok," she says, stepping back and frowning.

"Be careful how you speak to her," I warn, my voice quieter than it was before she entered the room. "And get out."

"We're not done, Conri," Felix growls. "This is unacceptable! You can't just–"

I hold up a hand, directing him to shut the fuck up if he knows what's good for him. "We will finish this discussion, Felix, in a minute. Get out."

"No! We need to talk, Jager!"

"And I said, we will. For now, though, you will get the fuck out of my office. I had a meeting scheduled to speak with Penelope before her shift begins, and poor management by you and your nephew does not constitute an emergency on my part. I will let you know when I am available."

Felix and Trevor both storm out of the office to the chagrin of Penelope and the amusement of Mike. My friend winks at her, then shuts the door behind them and takes his appointed place as guard.

"What happened?" she asks, rounding the desk and hopping up on it next to me. She crosses her legs, showing the red soles of the shoes I purchased for her and making her skirt ride up just enough to show the top of her thigh high stockings.

"Mmm," I hedge, running a hand up one of her thighs and gently spreading them apart. "Nothing important."

"Why was Trevor on the ground?"

"I hit him."

"Why?"

"To teach his uncle a lesson," I purr as I stand between her legs and lean down to nuzzle behind her ear. I thought I couldn't get enough of her before she gave herself to me. Now? She really is the sweetest addiction. "He destroyed the gift you gave me."

She gasps, both in distress and pleasure as I slip my fingers beneath her panties. "The crystal?" she asks, panting. "Did he drop it?"

"No." My fingers slip slowly inside her causing her to groan and lean back slightly, widening her legs to give me more room to work without my having to ask for it. "He threw it. So his nephew paid for it. Are you upset with me?"

"Up– upset? With you?"

"Mmmhmm." My pace picks up slightly as I shift my position so I can rub her clit with my thumb at the same time.

"I can't be upset with you when you touch me like this," she breathes, then pulls me toward her and seals her lips to mine, moaning softly and riding my hand like a starved woman. Most of me wants to drop my own pants and bury myself inside her to give her what she really needs, but my Poppy doesn't like to be late for work. The next time I fuck her I'm going to make it last.

"I need you to come for me so you can get to work, ok, Sweetness? I'll take better care of you later, I promise. Can you give me that? Can you come for me?"

"Yes. God, yes. Please."

I add another finger inside her and use my other hand to apply pressure to her clit, and mere moments later her body tenses and she releases a long, low moan that is so fucking sexy I almost come in my pants like a teenager.

Or Trevor.

I slow my movements to help her come down without feeling as if she's been thrown off a cliff, then suck my fingers into my mouth the second her eyes are able to focus enough to watch me.

"Good girl," I tell her, bending to press a kiss to her mouth. "What time is your first set?"

Her eyes widen with worry as soon as I mention time. "Shit!" I chuckle when she curses, loving the way it sounds falling from her innocent lips. "I'm going to be late!" She frantically attempts to get down from the desk but I'm blocking her way. I calmly readjust her panties so her beautiful pink pussy is covered, then grab her by the waist so I can place her gently on her feet as I step back.

"They'll manage." I take her hand and walk her to the door, then kiss her before opening it. "I'll have Cassie prepare my usual.."

"Thank you, Poppy," I tell her, gently snagging her hand before she can pull it back from the table. Holding still and silently demanding eye contact from her, once she meets my gaze I slowly lift it to my lips, turning it so her palm faces up. Instead of pressing a chaste kiss to the center as I'm sure she expects, I lick a hot trail through her palm and bite the heel.

Watching her pupils blow is one of the hottest fucking things I've ever seen.

Her breath catches and she pulls her bottom lip between her teeth, eyes widening in panic as she begins to shift slightly in place.

Is my little Poppy wet?

Now she has to perform while filled with need. For me.

Perfect.

"Um…" she hedges, breaking my gaze and frantically looking around as if she's going to get in trouble. As if I don't own this fucking place and anyone else actually has any say over what happens here.

I press a soft kiss to her palm and release her, nodding to show her it's ok to back up.

"Make them worship," I urge her, dropping the fingers that were just inside her into my drink to stir it, then taking a sip and relaxing back in my seat.

Her breath stutters as she realizes exactly what I'm doing, then takes a deep breath before looking to the left and seeing the smile on Mike's face. Her blush is beautiful, and she collects herself and gives me a nervous wave before hurrying to the door that leads backstage.

"Jesus, man," Mike laughs. "She's absolutely precious. I just can't figure out how she's so sweet in life, but so incredibly…" The growl I release makes him laugh even harder, but unlike anyone else he's too stupid to know when to stop while he's ahead. "Confident onstage. Don't come at me! You know I'm a one woman man. And she'd kill me." His fond smile as he thinks of Mina makes me wonder if I look like that when I think of Penelope. "Damn, you've got it bad."

Chapter Fifteen

"Penny, do you have a minute?"

Freaking Trevor!

I must not stab the man who gave me a job. Right? Especially since he just got beat up.

Right?

"Sure. Not long though, I have a set."

"I know, that's what we need to talk about."

Confused, I follow him into his office and take a seat in front of his desk. Funnily enough, all of the cameras are only showing completely appropriate angles like the entrances, bar, and other non-questionable areas.

"What's up, Trevor?"

"I wanted to see if you'd be interested in moving to another club."

"Another club?" I ask, confused. Why would I go somewhere else? Over the last few weeks I've become incredibly popular. I've even increased patronage and spending at the bar, according to Jager and Mina.

"Yeah. I know you didn't want to dance from the beginning. I've got another club where a spot for a bottle girl came available. I think you'd be great and you wouldn't have to worry about disappointing your Gran anymore."

"What?" I choke, completely offended and somewhat mortified.

"You told me from the start she'd be disappointed in you," he says. "Being a bottle girl wouldn't be as shameful."

"Shameful? What the fuck, Trevor?" He blinks at my use of the curse. I think it's the first time he's ever heard me say it. "You manage this place; is that what you really think about the girls who work here?"

"No, that's not what I think," he hedges. "But I really think you need to consider it."

"Why, then? I never said she would be ashamed of me, I said she'd wish I didn't feel like I needed to. That's a big difference! What is this really about?"

"It's about how much of a spectacle you're making of yourself!" he snaps, slamming his fist down on the top of his desk. "You're embarrassing yourself out there every fucking day, Penny! You're fawning over Conri like a lovesick little slut. He's going to drop you just like he has every other woman and you're going to be left looking like a whore and an idiot."

My jaw has to be on the floor at this point. I'm shocked he could ever say anything like that, let alone to me. I stand, turning my back on him and making my way to the door.

"Where are you going? Don't walk away from me when I'm talking to you!"

"You lost the right to speak to me, Trevor. First, because you can't respect the fact that I've asked you a thousand times NOT to call me Penny. Second, you called me a whore. The fact that I take my clothes off and dance for strangers doesn't make me or the other women here whores, Trevor. It makes us powerful. On top of that? How my Gran feels about me, and my relationship with Jager Conri, are none of your *fucking* business."

I have to hold back the angry tears that are threatening to fall. Darn excessive emotions!

The door opens and I'm almost completely through it when he fires his last shot.

"You're fired!"

I stop in my tracks and turn to look back at him, a smirk I only partially feel curving my lips.

"Wanna bet?"

JAGER

"Fuck off," I bark before rising from my booth and ignoring Mike's laugh.

He's not wrong, though.

He's not wrong about her being this stunning, perfect little dichotomy, and he's not wrong about me having it bad.

There are two young guys sitting at the table at the end of the stage where my little Poppy is about to perform, and that's not going to work for me. I step up next to them and simply stare, waiting for them to notice. When after thirty seconds they still haven't realized I'm standing next to them, I clear my throat.

"Move."

They both jump, as I timed my comment during a lull in the music.

"Fuck off, old man. We were here first!"

"Is that right?" I ask drolly.

"Yeah. We've been waiting for Ruby to come on for an hour! This bitch is fucking ho–"

Mike lunges to grab the idiot who has dared to refer to her as a bitch, but for once I'm the one who is too fast for him. The startled gurgle that he releases stops him in his tracks.

"Seriously, boss?"

"What? He's not dying. Yet."

"Holy shit! He stabbed me!"

"Shut up," Mike snarls, grabbing each of the kids by the collar and lifting them up in the air. The one who was dumb enough to talk back is clutching his side, trying to stem the flow of blood. He drags them out and I stand back, taking a sip of the drink my girl brought me a few minutes ago and waiting as a waitress scurries up to wipe the dark liquid from the floor and take away the sullied chair.

And after all that?

Didn't even spill a drop.

The quiet strains of *Rain* by Sleep Token begin, pumped out by the new sound system that was installed overnight, and I can immediately tell that something is wrong. Her posture, while normally upright and languid, is almost stiff and stunted. Like she's retreated inside herself for some reason. Don't get me wrong, she's still perfectly captivating. The entire room is silent and watching her as if they are as incapable as I am of taking their eyes off her, but there's a pain to her dance that is almost heartbreaking to watch.

As she tends to do with most dances, she's made her way down the runway to me for the climax of the song. Normally I allow her to tease the crowd by flirting with me, but not today. Not with that devastation reflecting in her eyes. I step to the edge of the stage and surprise her by cupping her cheek, and she freezes in place. Tears well, shimmering in time with the strobe lights that flash around us, and when she blinks they fall.

Not on my watch. Not like this.

I pull her to me and devour her sweet lips, reveling in the salty sweetness of her kiss. When she begins shaking I simply pull her from the stage and wrap her around me, carrying her away from the crowd to the sound of thunderous applause.

Mike is waiting at the door for us and holds it open for me to walk through as she begins to sob on my shoulder, my rage building with each tear, each sniffle, each step. I allow him to move past me and unlock my office door so we can enter, and he shuts it quietly behind me, locking it and no doubt staying in place.

No one will disturb us while I find out what happened.

Then I'll deal with it.

I take her over to the new couch that was finally delivered yesterday, and I adjust her position in my arms so she can comfortably curl up in my lap while she cries her heart out. I need her to stop, not only because she should never cry like this, but because I need to know who I'm about to fucking kill.

"Poppy," I call to her quietly, brushing her hair behind her ear to reveal some of her face. Her mascara is running so severely her cheeks are almost black. "Sweetness, talk to me." My questioning only causes her to cry harder, though, and the tissues are across the room on my desk. Unwilling to disturb her any further, I grab the end of my silk tie and do my best to wipe away the tears and smeared makeup from her face. It takes a second but she eventually realizes what I'm doing and jerks back from me, tears stopping as if they were the product of a faucet that was simply turned off at the tap.

"What are you doing?" she asks, snagging the fabric from my hand and using the palm of her other to try and wipe the black marks from the silk. "You've ruined it!"

"So?" I ask, unable to understand why that's a problem.

"So?" she repeats, horror on her face. Is that an improvement over sadness? "So?! It's real silk!"

"I don't care. What happened? Is something wrong with your Gran?"

"Gran is fine," she sniffles, still dabbing at the stain until I take it back from her and take the entire thing off and throw it across the room. "Jager, that tie has to have cost a fortune!"

"Fuck the tie," I growl, "What. Happened." I'm not asking anymore, I'm demanding. "Who hurt you?"

"Hurt me?" Shock is all I can find on her face now, not sadness. "No one hurt me."

"Penelope, I will not ask again. I'm about to lose my cool and go find anyone to take it out on. Please tell me what's upset you so I can fix it."

"Upset me?"

I sigh. "Yes. Please tell me what upset you, so I can fix it."

God, I feel like such a jerk! Jager is truly worried about me, and here I am making him do it unnecessarily! I bury my face in his chest for a second, not worried about my mascara anymore because unlike his tie, his shirt is black.

"I'm not sad, I'm pissed," I mumble, letting his cologne surround and calm the last of my frayed nerves. When he asks me to repeat myself, I know I need to toughen up and admit what's really going on, no matter the consequences.

"I said, I'm not sad. I'm angry."

The confusion and complete disbelief in his eyes is the final thing I needed to release the grip the tears held on me. "But you're crying."

"I know!"

"Penelope," he says, voice stern. "Tell me."

Ugh. Now I'm mad *and* horny!

"I'm angry, ok?" I blurt. "I can't help it. I'm a rage cryer." I can tell he's not following and has already lost his patience with being unable to figure out what's going on, so I rush to try to explain. "It's something I can't help! When I get really, really mad, and I know I can't do anything about it, it leaks out of my eyes." I shrug, trying to play it down. "I'm sorry. I didn't mean to worry you. I just haven't been this angry in a long time and I couldn't hold it back."

"Why can't you do anything about it?"

I shrug again. I'm super articulate tonight.

"Because stabbing people just for saying mean things isn't healthy. Or legal."

"Debatable," he quips, a small smile quirking the corner of his mouth. "Penelope, what happened?"

"You have to promise to let me handle it," I insist, holding up a finger in warning. I'm highly skeptical he'll agree, but I have to try.

"I can't do that."

Called it.

"Please," I beg. "It's important to me. No one physically hurt me or did anything you can fix."

"I will try," he grits out. "But I can't promise."

"I guess that's fair. It was Trevor."

"Did he touch you?"

"No! No. He... well, he called me into his office before my last set. He offered me a job at another club doing bottle service. He basically said doing that would be less shameful and embarrassing."

"He said... what?" His voice sounds deadly, and while it's terrifying, it's also sexy as heck.

Fuck. It's sexy as *fuck*.

"When we first discussed the job I told him I didn't want Gran to know. I only said that because she didn't want me working at all, and because she stripped when she was younger."

"She did?" He actually looks somewhat impressed, and I give him a quick kiss of thanks.

"Yeah. And she loved it, but she started it out of necessity. She never wanted me to be in a position where I felt like I was so desperate that I had to do it. She loved that I was taking lessons from Halla, and was proud of the talent I showed for it, but I just don't think she'd believe I was doing this because I wanted to, not because I had to. She's already so sick and needs help with her care; I'm terrified of her feeling like a financial burden, too."

"There is nothing for you to feel ashamed about, Penelope Channing. You may have taken this job out of necessity instead of a desire to do it, but you became a headliner here practically overnight because of your talent. Not because of me, or Trevor, or anything else. It was all you."

This time the tear that falls isn't from anger. It's from the absolutely overwhelming amount of love I feel for this man who is so tough for everyone else, but doesn't hesitate to show that he has the most caring heart.

"Now," he says, wiping away the tear. "I'm going to let you handle this. For now. But if it escalates further I will handle him."

"Noted," I tell him, smiling my thanks.

"In the meantime..."

"In the meantime?"

"You have a set soon, although I will enjoy seeing your mascara run when you're choking on my cock, this is different. I know you'll want to clean up. Besides–"

"Besides what?"

Instead of answering me immediately, he lifts and repositions me so I'm straddling him then lifts my skirt until it's around my waist. Grabbing the sides of my bright red g-string, he meets my eyes as he rips and tosses it aside.

"The only thing running out of you should be my cum."

I'm shocked into speechlessness for a fraction of a second, then I simply lift his arm so I can check the time on his watch.

Wincing, I turn his hand over and kiss his palm. "I have to be back on stage in thirty minutes, and I still need to clean up and get ready."

His smile flashes larger than I've ever seen it as his hands begin caressing my body. "I guess I need to be quick then."

I picture him laying me out on the desk and ravishing me like we're on the set of some old soap opera until Trevor calling me a slut and a whore flashes through my mind. I begin to fall into that anger and sorrow again, but I force myself to shut it down immediately.

I am neither of those things.

I am a woman who is strong, confident, and coming into my own.

I'm not stupid. Trevor has had a crush on me since we were kids. So, in his mind, because I don't want him back, there's something wrong with me? Something dirty or shameful?

Fuck him, and fuck anyone who thinks that way. No one is obligated to return affection or desire, and I won't allow him to make me feel like less simply because he wants more. I won't allow anyone to control who and what I am, or who and what I want.

Because for the first time in my life, I *know* what I want.

I want *this* man, and I'm so incredibly lucky that he also wants me.

Chapter Sixteen

I reach down and quickly free him from his pants, giggling when he eagerly lifts up just enough so I can pull them down and feel his skin against mine. He moves to touch me, but I don't want any foreplay this time, I just need to have him inside me. I take him into my hand and stroke him firmly, showing him I'm not messing around, then rise up on my knees. With our height difference I'm still only at eye level with him, but that's ok. I love how small he makes me feel, but when I try to angle him inside me, I'm not tall enough for him to fit. Instead of helping me, though, I shriek in surprise as he wraps me up and flips us so I'm laid back on the couch and he's leaning over me.

"Gravity," he murmurs, "that won't work."

"What won't?" I ask as he takes over completely and spreads my thighs as wide as they can comfortably go. My pussy is completely exposed to him and I suppress another giggle as his tongue traces his bottom lip as if he's debating tasting me again.

"Hey," I call, snapping my fingers in his face and gaining his reluctant attention. "I have to work, remember? If you start licking my pussy I'll never make my set on time."

"Quit."

"Jager Conri!" I scold. "You either fuck me right now or I'm leav—"

My words are cut short when he slams inside me, turning my fake threat into a real gasp of pleasure/pain. I'm still not used to it, but the sensation of the most intimate pieces of our bodies coming together is absolute bliss.

"You're not going anywhere," he growls, each word punctuated by a thrust. "Not until I'm done with you, and I'll *never* be done."

A fact that he spends the next twenty minutes proving to me. My years of ballet and pole work serve me well as he pushes my body as far as the office loveseat we're occupying will allow. He spreads me wide and positions me in ways that I, if I had time to think, would have thought would bring only discomfort, but instead only intensify the mind numbing pleasure he's giving me. I've just been lifted into the air and positioned with my back on the cushion and my butt propped up on the arm when Jager slows his thrusts to a pace that's so abruptly different my brain practically short circuits.

"Now, Sweetness, you're going to come for me again."

"Again?" I yelp. "I already did. A few times!"

"Again. You only have," he raises his arm to look at his watch, "fourteen minutes before you go onstage, and you have to get ready."

"Shit! Jager, I have to go!"

"You *have* to come," he orders, licking his thumb and placing it against my clit as he begins to speed up his thrusts once more.

"But what about you?"

"Don't worry about me, I made you a promise."

"What promise?" I ask, entranced by the sight of his cock sliding in and out of me while his thumb draws lazy circles.

He doesn't answer, only shushes me and leans forward far enough to wrap his other hand around my throat and press against me slightly. I can still breathe, but the partial restriction only works to intensify all other sensations. My third orgasm of the night doesn't just build, it explodes out of me without any warning and I scream my release as much as possible without full lungs.

Jager grunts, his forehead creasing in concentration as he watches where we're joined and his grip tightens around my throat even further. With a dissatisfied grunt, he moves his other hand from my clit to grip the outside of my left thigh so tightly it's as if he's holding on for dear life. His pace and force both increase until all I can do is stretch one arm out over my head and brace against the other end of the loveseat to keep from being pushed away from him. I use the other to give him the best of both worlds and begin to play with my clit while he watches. The crease in his forehead somehow seems to turn from one of frustration to one of concentration, and I know he's trying to come for me, just like he asked me to come for him.

So I ask.

"Please," I breathe, "Jager, I need you to come inside me." His eyes jerk to mine and I can't help but smile as his rhythm hitches briefly. I use his momentary distraction to wrap my legs around him and roll my hips up to meet him. "I need to dance soon, remember? Come for me so I can leave you running down my thighs while others watch. Watch me touch myself and claim me so spectacularly in front of the world that Trevor will never even consider bothering me again."

Apparently that did it, because he drops his gaze back to where our bodies meet. I speed up my movements and time the thrust of my hips to his and do my best to squeeze his cock with my inner muscles. Less than a minute later he finally groans out his release, squeezing me harder and almost cutting my air off completely. My eyelids begin to flutter closed as I feel him pulse within me, and I welcome it when he almost collapses at my side, pulling me against him and kissing my forehead as we both work to catch our breath.

I snag his hand again and look at his watch, gasping when I see there's only seven minutes until I'm supposed to be on stage.

"Shit! I have to get cleaned up!" I yelp, frantically trying to untangle myself from him and pull my skirt down far enough to get down the hallway. I look around for my panties and then remember he destroyed them and gasp, flinging myself backward on the couch once more. Maybe I can just... not dance this time?

"What's wrong?" he asks lazily, standing and casually tucking himself back into his pants. Freaking men. He looks like he's fresh from the shower while I probably look like I've been rode hard and put up wet.

Which, I guess, is an accurate statement.

But still.

"You destroyed my panties!" I scold, my heart only half in it.

"I did."

"I don't have any extras here tonight!"

"So?"

"So?" Seriously? This man is infuriating sometimes! "I am about to dance on stage. I know you like to watch other people want me, but do you really want a club full of strangers to see my ejaculate filled pussy?" He pauses, considering, and he's lucky he decides that the answer is no. "Not only is that *illegal* in this state," I remind him, "but as much as I'm willing to try new things that is where I draw the line."

"Good," he nods. "I'll have Mina check for a clean pair."

"Gross! I'm not wearing someone else's panties, Jager. Regardless of whether they've been washed."

"They're not used," he chuckles, rolling his eyes. "I purchased them for you and had them laundered, but I'm not sure if they've been delivered yet." He moves to his desk and dials an extension, leaving it on speakerphone so I can hear the conversation.

"Yes, Mr. Conri?" Mina asks, voice as sweet as ever.

"Mina, I need the white outfit at Penelope's station immediately if it's here. She also may need assistance touching up her makeup. She is running late and goes on in five."

"No problem!" she chirps happily. "She's so naturally beautiful that she doesn't need much help, isn't she?"

"She is," he answers, unabashed, making my heart flutter. I love how this strong, aggressive man has no hesitation in showing or telling people how he feels about me.

"Anything else, sir? The clothing was delivered yesterday so it's all ready to go."

"Please have Cassie fill my order and have it waiting at my table, and we'll be there in one minute. Please have her items ready."

"You got it!"

He presses the button to hang up the call and walks over to where I'm still sprawled out on the loveseat, reaching his hand down to help me stand. "Let's get you ready."

"I can do it myself," I grumble as I take his offered hand.

"What are these?" I squeak, looking at the practically sheer white g-string on the hanger next to my station and quickly but reluctantly pulling them on. Freaking man was right. Gravity is a bitch after sex, apparently.

"Your outfit for this next dance," he tells me, fingering the netting of the corset. "I may not want the room to see your pretty pussy, but you weren't wrong when you said I like to watch. This way, I can see how wet my cum is making you. And your panties."

"But so can everyone else!" I whine, accepting the corset from him and allowing Mina to come up behind me and tie it up while I do my best to fix my hair and makeup. My motions pause, however, as I freshen up my lipstick. "You know what? That's actually perfect. I'm ok here, I'll finish getting ready. You should go get your seat so you don't miss anything."

Suspicious clouds his eyes. "You better not be going to the bathroom right now," he warns. I laugh, standing on my tiptoes to give him a kiss goodbye before I sit to put my shoes on.

"I'm not, I promise. Let's just say, this performance is going to be a little different."

He looks like he's going to argue, but instead he checks his watch then barks one last order. "Mina, do not allow her to use the restroom."

"You got it!" she responds, dropping to the ground to fasten my shoes and refusing to look up until he's gone for fear of letting him see the mirth behind her pretty eyes.

"What in the world?" she asks. "Did he really?" She widens her eyes and points at my crotch, then makes an explosion noise and motion with her hands. I laugh so hard it can only be considered a cackle, but immediately stop because I can feel things... shift.

"Yes," I grumble. "And he won't let me go to the bathroom before I go on. But I'm going to use that to my advantage because I've got some revenge that needs to be served out. Can you do me a favor?"

"Anything in the name of revenge!" she cheers as she jumps up and down, clapping happily. "Lay it on me."

Chapter Seventeen

For this dance, I'm not even bothering with the outfit that was purchased to go with the lingerie. I simply take my position on stage with a plain trench coat wrapped around me, the belt loosely tied. Mina instructed the DJ to turn off all non-emergency lights in the club proper before I stepped on stage, and she had Mike make sure Trevor was out there as well. With everything that happened, we only started four minutes late, and that was only because the extra song the DJ played had to finish.

As the lights turn off without warning the patrons and staff all gasp, and Trevor goes into his "I'm the manager and I'm in charge mode," rushing around and calling out for people to figure out what's going on. My attention is focused on the man at the end of the stage, though, only a faint silhouette visible in the barely-there lighting. As I expected, he doesn't move other than to take a sip of his drink.

I instructed Mina to tell the DJ once he heard my heel click twice on the stage floor to slowly start turning the lights back up as a man begins telling people that there are whores in the house. The chatter immediately stops as the patrons realize I'm about to start my set without being announced.

Surprise!

"WAP" by Cardi B feat Megan Thee Stallion turns up, and though I'm already spinning through the air on the pole when the lights are up high enough for me to be seen by everyone, I make it a point to try to see Jager's face.

It's worth every fucking moment of discomfort.

He looks just as uncomfortable with the music that's playing as I do with my wet panties and it's everything I can do not to laugh while I'm facing the back of the club! I quickly pull it together though and drop back to the floor after a few rotations. I'm fairly certain none of them are sure what's going on, because I've never danced to anything other than rock music. This could not be any further from what I'm known for.

I quickly ditch my coat and am left in nothing but a g-string, balconette bra, fishnet thigh highs, and clear heels. I dance to the music, giving Jager a show and ready to prove to Trevor how much of a *whore* I really can be.

He's not going to enjoy that very much, but I will.

Spinning on the pole feels a little... slippier than normal as I slide back down, but I make do. I can feel a faint trail of moisture left behind from where I was able to grind my pussy into it, and it makes me smile to think that Jager's cum is not only claiming me right now, it's essentially claiming the entire club, too.

Poor Trevor.

I have no intention of telling Trevor, though I sort of hope he notices. I do, however, make a mental note to let Mina know it should probably be disinfected before the next performer goes on.

I make my way to the end of the stage, dropping into the splits in front of Jager and blowing mental kisses to the DJ when the lights turn from gel to black lighting the second I hit the floor. This is going to give what he's about to see so much more... impact.

I pull my legs together and move to sit with them bent in front of me, leaning them over to one side when my attention is grabbed by a dark spot against my shining skin. It was exciting enough to think the blacklight would show the evidence of what we'd just done on the pole and my panties, but this revelation is even better. I smile and meet Jager's waiting gaze as he continues to watch me, then stretch out my left leg in front of him and caress my skin where the perfect imprint of his hand shows in dim comparison to the bright white of the stockings. His eyes take it in and he leans back, licking his bottom lip and letting me know I'm going to get more where that came from later.

Say less.

I finally straighten to pull my heels to my butt for a moment then lean back on one hand and again move into the splits. This time, though, instead of a normal split my legs create a wide "V" in the air and frame my glowing wet pussy right in front of his expectant face. The crowd goes wild for me when I run my fingers down my chest, stomach, and then dip them below the scrap of fabric Jager calls panties to collect a bit of the moisture there. I wasn't planning on doing that, but when I saw the arousal in his eyes at the sight of my damp pussy, I couldn't help myself.

I jump and jerk my fingers back out when Trevor storms up behind Jager, his face lined with rage and his fists balled tight, but luckily Mike stops him before he can get to the table. For a moment I'm back in that room with him calling me a whore, but when Jager stands and steps up to the edge of the stage? All of that disappears. The pumping music helps drown out the argument, and the world narrows down to Jager, the bass, and me. He briefly looks down at my fingers, held awkwardly in front of me, then jerks his chin at my mouth to tell me what he wants.

Remembering I'm back on stage, I begin dancing to the music once again, knowing the song is almost over and wanting this last part to be just for us. The second the song dies and the lights with it? I'm facing Jager once more and I slip my fingers in my mouth, groaning at the feel and taste of the two of us combined.

Maybe there really *are* hoes in this house, because he makes me feel like one.

In the best way.

Chapter Eighteen – Gran

The doorbell rings, startling me and causing me to miss the clue that nailed the murderer on my ID channel show. Who the fuck could that be at this time of night? The bell rings again, and now I'm just irritated. I'm a frail, cancer riddled old lady, damnit! Give me a chance to get my sick ass up off the couch.

"I'm coming, keep your pants on!" I yell after the third time the bell is rung. It figures someone would come by on the one damn night I'm feeling good enough to not need the night nurse.

"What?" I snap, throwing the door open and getting even more irritated that it's not the police or someone equally important. Some scrawny guy is here, looking familiar but I can't quite place him. I guess he's just got one of those faces that aren't all that memorable.

"Ms. Channing?"

"Yes? Who are you again? Why are you here so late? Penelope isn't here."

"Yes, ma'am, I actually know. I'm Trevor? We met at lunch a few months back and I gave Penny a job?"

"Penelope," I correct him automatically. That's right. He couldn't remember that she hated him calling her that then, and he apparently can't remember it now.

"Right, sorry."

"So why are you here if you know she's out?"

"I wanted to speak with you, actually."

"Why?" What on Earth could he have to talk to me about?

"Well, I'm worried about her."

I sigh, seeing the truth of his words in his face. "Alright, come on in. Tell me what's going on."

He thanks me and follows me into the kitchen where I offer him a glass of water and sit down at the table with him and my own glass.

"It's Mr. Conri, I'm afraid."

"What about him?"

"Well, I'm worried he's abusing her. He's taking advantage of her and making her..."

"He's making her what?" I ask, my already unsettled stomach dropping into my toes.

"He's making her dance," he hedges. "You know, strip."

"She's stripping?"

"Yes, ma'am. Penelope swore me to silence, but I just can't keep it quiet anymore. It's not right."

"It's not right that she's stripping?" I ask him. "Why not?"

"Oh, um... I don't mean there's anything wrong with it. I just think that she must think it's wrong if she didn't want you to know about it, you know? And he's making her be his personal waitress, and controlling everything she does! I don't think she's safe with him, Ms. Channing. She's losing who she is as a person and doing things she normally wouldn't."

Penny

Dont wait up I have 2 wrk 2nite now

"What in the world?" I mutter, having to read the text Penny just sent me at least five times to understand what it says. She always texts like she speaks, she doesn't use the number 2 to replace the word, and she never forgets an apostrophe.

Is she drunk?

Wait, he's having her work and she's typing like that?

"Is everything ok?" Trevor asks, oozing fake concern.

"I just got a strange text from her. She said she has to work tonight, but she's supposed to be going out to dinner and the opera with Jager."

"See! That's why I'm here! I was just about to tell you that. He's making her dance again tonight instead of doing what he promised! He changed the schedule last minute so she's got multiple sets tonight with no notice. She's also having to waitress on top of that. It's like he doesn't care what she's going through unless it's making him money. Or making him look good!"

That truly doesn't sound like the man I've met, but you can never really be certain with these things. He's a bit domineering, but it sounds to me like they have an understanding. I don't think he's a man who would go back on his promises, but my Penny also isn't one to turn down work — she's worried about our finances and she hates being sedentary.

"Give me five minutes."

"What do you mean?"

"I'm packing a good dinner for my girl, since she isn't going to the one she was expecting, and I'll find out what's going on. There's only one way to do that."

"How?"

"I need to be there and see for myself."

He puts up a token argument with me, telling me he promised her that he wouldn't tell me, but his heart isn't truly in it. He wants me to come and get things straight.

But why? Is he in love with her or something? Maybe he's more worried than a normal friend or employer would be because he has feelings for her.

I grab my old picnic basket, throw in some of the prepared meals that Conri had delivered, and dress in something other than my pajamas, which is a nice change if I'm being honest. I feel like I've been nothing but a slob lately.

"Ready," I tell him with my basket hooked over my arm. "Let's go talk to her."

"If you'll just wait here I'll go grab her," Trevor tells me, gesturing to a chair on the opposite side of a desk with a crapload of monitors showing the entrances of the building on the wall behind it.

"I can go find her, you don't need to worry about me."

"I'm going to go find her and let her know you came to surprise her with dinner, if that's ok. I'd rather she not find out I went to speak with you."

"I understand," I tell him. "Thank you, Trevor."

He nods and exits the room, shutting the door behind me. The lock clicks quietly, as if he was trying to keep me from noticing the sound. What the hell? I toss the heavy basket onto the desk and rush to the door as fast as I can, which is admittedly not very fast right now, and try the knob.

Locked!

Why would he lock me in here? I'm an old woman, not a sexual predator.

I bang on the door for a minute but nothing happens, and I can't hear anyone on the other side when I press my ear to it. Grumbling, I turn around and head to the basket, rummaging around until I can find a butterknife. It may not be sharp, but at least it's something to attempt to protect myself with if things go that way. I look up, blowing my thinning hair out of my face and freeze.

The camera angles have changed and they're all showing recorded footage of Penny. I'm guessing it's from different nights because they're all in different locations in the club and she's wearing different outfits.

She's on stage performing. She's giving lap dances. She's changing in the changing room!

This motherfucker!

I knew something wasn't right from the second I opened the door! Is Penny even here? Looking around I notice two other doors in the room. The bi-fold door opens to a small closet, and the other opens to a small, disgusting bathroom. I cannot even imagine what that man does in there, especially with these videos of Penny playing all at once!

Realizing I'm stuck in here, I decide to go back to the videos and learn all I can. She's dancing, and I truly look at her. Everywhere but the changing room, at least. She looks beautiful up there. Much more talented than I ever was, and she looks like she's truly enjoying herself. I don't obseve any discomfort, fear, or upset on her face, only something close to euphoria. Just like I used to feel.

Jager isn't forcing my girl to do anything! Why would Trevor lie to me, though?

Actually, I don't care why. All I care about is that he's lying to me, and I'm pissed that the little shit is filming her and watching it all back later. My grip tightens on my pathetic weapon as I take in the screens, and I debate the merits of putting the knife through his eye versus up his stupid fucking nose that he can't keep out of my granddaughter's business.

"You weren't supposed to see that," comes a voice I don't recognize. I spin around and find Trevor and a greasy looking middle aged man dripping with what looks to be fake gold jewelry.

"Who the hell are you? Trevor, what in the fuck is this?" I demand, gesturing to the monitors with my knife.

"Wow, grandma's spicy," the unknown man chuckles.

"Spicy? You have no idea. You have two seconds to tell me what the fuck is really going on here before I shove this up your nose, Trevor. Start talking!"

Trevor puts his hands up in a placating gesture, talking slowly and quietly as if he's trying not to spook a rabbit. I may be a cancer filled grandmother, but I am not a rabbit. I'm a fucking lioness and they're going to learn just how much they picked the wrong people to mess with. My Penny may be a sweet and soft girl, but most of that takes effort on her part. She's just like me, after all.

You mess with the people we love? We'll burn the fucking world to ash.

Just ask the dealer who gave my daughter bad drugs.

Oh, what's that? He can't answer?

Probably because my husband cut his tongue out before we killed him for taking her away from us. Penny may not realize it, but she's got that same fire inside of her, and I think these two are about to spark it.

"I know this looks weird, Ms. Channing, but it isn't what you think. These are just quality assurance videos. We play back videos of all of our dancers to make sure they're doing their jobs and our clients are happy. You just happened upon her review for the week."

"In the changing room? What does that have to do with how she dances for clients?"

"It doesn't," the other man chortles. "Trevor here just has a thing for her. He watches her more than he needs to."

"Shut up, Uncle Felix!" Travor snaps, shoving his uncle in warning. Just as quickly, he turns back to me, pleading. "That's not true, I swear."

"Bullshit. Something is wrong here and it's going to stop! Now where is my granddaughter? I'm getting her out of this place!"

Trevor's face instantly changes from desperate to enraged, causing me to take a step back.

"You're not fucking taking her anywhere! You have one job, you old bitch, to get her away from Conri!"

"Old bitch?" I scoff, "You have no idea how big of a bitch I can be. Don't fuck with me you little runt, you have no idea who you're messing with." I turn to grab my basket off his desk and exit the room, but the moment I have the basket in hand a blow to the back of my knee drops me so quickly I fall forward and slam my head on the desk. Rolling, I fall over to the side into a heap on the ground. My head is instantly on fire, a warm, thick liquid that I can only assume is blood trickling down my forehead.

"Why couldn't you just do what you were supposed to?" he screams, stepping forward and kicking me in the stomach so hard that at least one of my ribs snaps.

"Please," I whimper when a cough produces blood. "Please stop."

"No! You were supposed to come here and save her from that fucking asshole!" he yells, spittle flying from his mouth and landing on my face. "You were supposed to make her fall for me! But you had to put your nose where it doesn't belong, didn't you? You had to get in the way!"

"I... will..."

"Trevor, does Penny know she's here?"

"No. Not yet."

Oh, God. They're going to kill me, aren't they?

"Good. I've got an idea."

Cheap, designer knockoff shoes enter my line of sight and I cringe, knowing the final blow is about to come. They can't afford to let me live. Not now.

Just like I expect, one of the feet lifts and connects with my head. The thought that Jager will protect my girl is the last thought I can manage.

Then everything goes black.

Chapter Nineteen

"**W**hat?" Jager barks when his phone rings the third time. He's ignored the last two calls from Trevor, but now that he's called three times in as many minutes my only worry is that everything is not ok. He listens for a moment and the irritation grows the more he listens.

"Speed it up, Trevor. She's here, what do you want? Fine."

Instead of handing me the phone he hits the speakerphone button and places it on the table between us.

"Hello?" I ask, uncertain why anyone would be calling Jager for me.

"Penny? Thank God!" Trevor's voice reaches me, tinny and shaking with what sounds like stress.. I'm off tonight and for once instead of staying home I agreed to dinner with Jager since Gran was feeling well enough to watch her "murder shows" before an early bedtime.

I sigh. "Trevor, please."

"Sorry, I'm just a little frazzled."

"What's up?" I ask, giving Jager a questioning look. He simply raises an eyebrow and takes a sip of his drink.

"Um, well, your Gran is here."

"What?" I yelp in shock. Why would she be at the club?

"Your Gran is here. She said she thought you were working so she wanted to bring you dinner tonight. She also said she's been trying to call you but couldn't get through. Do you want me to take her home?"

"No," Jager answers for me as I jump and begin searching through my small handbag for my phone. It's not here!

"Penn– elope?

"No, thank you Trevor. We're on our way now."

Jager hangs up the phone and takes cash out of his wallet, dropping it on the table to cover the meal we hadn't even received yet.

"Jager, I can't find my phone! Do you think it's in my coat, or the car? I don't think I used it when we stopped by the club, did I?"

We quickly arrive at the coat check where he gives the woman a hundred dollar bill to retreive my coat immediately, much to the irritation of the patrons that were waiting before us.

"I think you texted to tell her we'd be later than planned since you agreed to a nightcap after the opera."

"Maybe I left it on your desk or something," I muse when a search of my coat pockets comes up empty. "Jager, she knew we were going to dinner tonight, and she's never brought me dinner before. She knew I wasn't working. Do you think... I don't know, do you think the chemo is messing with her cognition?"

"I don't know, Sweetness. We're only ten minutes from the club, though, so we'll find out quickly. Maybe she's just having a rougher night than we all thought and she's not feeling well. Sometimes that can cause confusion. I'll have a nurse meet us at the club to check her out."

"Thank you," I sigh, snuggling into his side as he leads me to the waiting car. "What did I do to deserve you?"

"I ask myself the same of you every day."

The ride is hell, but Mike could tell I was nervous so he ended up making it there in six minutes. I hop out of the car when we arrive at the club's rear entrance and Trevor and Felix are both there waiting for us. "Where is she?" I ask, frantic.

"This way," he tells me, beginning to lead me down the hallway.

"Conri," I hear Felix call out. "A minute?"

I look back over my shoulder as I follow Trevor and simply nod. I can handle Gran for now.

Trevor stops outside his office door and puts one hand on the knob and the other to his lips, telling me she'd fallen asleep a few minutes ago, then slowly opens it and allows me inside. The lights are on a dimmer, and the monitors are all turned off for once.

"She brought the picnic basket?" I ask, whispering. At his nod, I shake my head in confusion.

"What's wrong?"

"I don't know," I hedge. "She knew I wasn't working tonight. I'm worried that the treatment is affecting her mentally, though that would be something new if it is." I sigh and head to his desk to collect the basket before waking Gran to take her home.. "Sorry, Trevor. Thanks for calling me."

Footsteps sound out behind me and I turn toward the door, ready to ask Mike or Jager to help carry Gran to the car, when I notice two things.

First, Trevor is the one stomping toward me.

Second, Gran is unconscious, bleeding, and tied up.

My scream is so loud it actually stops Trevor in place for a fraction of a beat, but after looking back at the now closed door he collects himself and continues his charge toward me. Fuck that!

"Jager!"

"Shut up!" Trevor yells, reaching out to try and grab me. He must have forgotten self defense was mandatory for girls in high school, though, because I easily free myself from his grip on my arms and slam my heel down on his foot and shove him.

Hard.

He shouts in surprise as he stumbles backward, arms flailing as he tries to catch his balance but fails. He finally falls, slamming his head into the wall and leaving a dent there when he rolls away.

"Penelope!"

"In here! Jager, hurry!" I grab a butterknife I noticed glinting on the floor and drop to my knees in front of Gran, trying to use the dull blade to cut the tape away from her hands and feet. Trevor is dazed but trying to sit up, scrambling more frantically as the door begins to shake as if it's being rammed. Seconds later that thought is proven correct when Mike busts through it and both he and Jager enter with guns drawn and quickly clear the room. Mike stands over Trevor, kicking him in the stomach and telling him not to move, and Jager grabs me and pulls me into his arms.

It isn't until I've buried my face into his jacket that I realize I've been crying. Apparently, he noticed it before I did.

"Sadness, or rage?" he mumbles into my hair.

"What?" I lean back and look at him, trying to figure out what he's talking about.

"Are these tears sadness, or rage? I need to know."

"Oh," I breathe, collecting myself and stepping back before snarling, "Rage. I'm going to kill this bitch!"

"Not so fast," comes another voice from the broken doorway. I try to look around Jager's chest to see who is whimpering next to Felix, but he holds me tightly to him. Slowly and as unobtrusively as possible, Jager drops his gun hand to my side where the full skirt of my dress hides a pocket and slips his weapon inside so his hands are free.

I look at Mike since I can't see around Jager's shoulder and the blood drains from me as his face blanches. He immediately lifts his gun as he growls, "Motherfucker, think really hard about this, because it is the last thing you will ever fucking do. My word on that."

"Your word doesn't mean shit, Mikey," Felix gloats. I finally peek around Jager's shoulder and find him holding Mina to him with a gun to her head. She's bruised and bleeding, and it looks like the only reason she's even standing is that Felix is holding her by the hair. "Drop the gun, now. You too, Jager, and face me."

"Don't do it, Mikey," Mina mumbles, being brave even in the face of the pain she's going through.

"Now!" Felix shouts, cocking the gun and pushing it harder against her head, causing her to whimper again. "And get on your knees, both of you. Hands behind your head."

I can tell it's against everything in both of them to obey, but Mina is Mike's world, so they do. While Mike drops to his knees and places his gun on the ground in front of him, Jager simply raises his hands and shows that he's unarmed.

"Bullshit, Conri! You're never without a gun!"

"Not tonight, we were going to the opera and had security."

"Just… fine. Don't move. Mike, gently slide the gun over to Tr–"

Not allowing Felix to finish his sentence, Mike forcefully slides the gun to the opposite side of the room and away from both Felix and Trevor.

"Fucking try me!" Felix bellows, pissed that even though he has the gun in this situation he will never truly have the power. "Andre, get in here!"

Andre? I have no idea who Andre is, but Jager and Mike seem to because they still when an older gentleman walks into the room flanked by multiple men. Felix smiles.

"Fuck you, Conri. Andre, have one of your guys check him. I don't trust that he doesn't have a weapon on him."

"I do have a weapon, you fucking idiot. I never said I didn't. You told me to drop my gun."

One of the men with Andre slowly approaches Jager and respectfully requests permission to check him for weapons. Jager nods, informing him where his knives are concealed. The man takes them and finishes the pat down, then steps away and nods to Andre, who nods at Felix in turn.

"You think you're the only one with money, Jager? I sent Andre here a video of your little whore and he couldn't arrive fast enough to get his hands on the hot little slut. I don't need your money anymore, because I'm about to have his."

Fear grips me so strongly I'm almost paralyzed, this time for myself. Felix sold me? What will this man do to me? Who the fuck is he?

Trevor has finally regained his bearings and has stood up, slowly making his way to stand next to Felix and Mina.

"Is that so?" Jager asks, voice colder and quieter than I've ever heard it as he steps next to me and wraps an arm around my waist.

"Conri," Andre finally speaks up while looking me up and down with an expression I can't quite pinpoint. "I am sorry it came to this, but I was presented with a very... interesting opportunity."

"See, Penny?" Trevor croaks as he rubs his head. "He can't protect you! I can now. Just come here and we'll work this out." He extends a hand to me but I don't move, instead curling further into Jager's side. It looks like I'm cowering into him in fear, but I'm finally past that. As I look at Mina and Gran's injuries, Mike kneeling on the ground, and these men who are obviously here to hurt the man I love, I'm even past rage tears.

Now I'm just going to fucking kill them all.

I use his body and the volume of my skirt to hide my movements as I slip my hand into the hidden pocket he placed the gun in.

"Come here, Penny," Felix jeers. "Now. Or I kill Mina."

"I'm..." I fake a deep, terrified breath. "I'm coming." I look up to Jager and flick my eyes to where they stand, asking him if I should be brave enough to truly try to kill them. He smiles and caresses my face with the hand on the side facing them, then bends to me as if he's going to kiss my cheek goodbye. Instead, he whispers something part encouragement, part warning.

"The safety is off. Be careful."

Chapter Twenty

Jager stays by my Gran, standing over her like a sentinel, while I slowly walk over to Trevor, Felix, and poor Mina with both hands tucked in the folds of my dress.

"Let them go now."

"What?" Felix laughs incredulously.

"I'm over here now. Let my Gran and Mina go. You don't need them."

Trevor steps up next to me and tries to convince me to leave the room with him to talk, but I'm not leaving without the people I care about.

"I'm not kidding Felix. I don't care who is in here! Let my Gran and Mina go get some medical help now or–"

"Or what?" he asks, mocking me.

"Or I'll make you regret it. I can promise you that."

"What are you going to do, Penny? Shove your little 'WAP' in my face?"

"Nope."

"So wh–"

Trevor falls back into the wall once more when the gunshot rings out and his uncle's blood and brain matter spray all over us and the surrounding area.

"That's what I'll do, you fucking asshole!" I yell, turning and pointing my gun now at Andre since Trevor turned and ran out of the room screaming as soon as he collected himself enough to do so. Mike jumps up from his position and runs to Mina's side, but she scolds him strongly enough that he takes off after Trevor and catches him within seconds.

"Poppy?" Jager calls, wrapping one arm around my back and pulling me close.

"Yes?"

"What would you think about dropping the gun?"

"I'd think that's stupid because this guy just fucking bought me!"

"Penelope."

"What?" I snap, getting irritated.

"Give me the gun, Sweetness. I promise, it's ok. Andre is a friend, and I'm sure he has a very good explanation for being here."

"He's your friend?"

"Yes. I promise, if his explanation isn't good enough for you we'll kill him together, ok?"

Andre's brow lifts at this, and his men attempt to step in front of him, but he waves them back. I take a deep breath, hold it, then let it out slowly before dropping the gun and handing it back to Jager as Mike literally drags an unconscious Trevor back into the office.

"Can we please take care of Gran and Mina first?"

Thankfully, the nurse that Jager had called for on our drive over arrived shortly after we got them to the Quiet Room. Additionally, Gran had remained unconscious through the entire event but woke soon after. After hearing about what happened and being assured she was fine other than a headache, I felt safe enough in leaving her with Mina and the nurse. I needed to speak with Jager and Andre, but only after I got a list of every injury that had been inflicted on both of them.

Somehow I even got Mina to admit that the reason she can't dance anymore is because Felix was careless in the past and entered into a bad business deal and that shady partner took his disappointment out on Mina when Felix wasn't available. She lost her ability to dance, but she'd gained a percentage of the club ownership and met Mike through that awful event. According to her, she'd go through it all over again just to be with him.

When I arrive back at Jager's office I'm surprised to find him and Andre laughing together, and it almost shocks me to realize they truly are friends.

"Penelope," Jager smiles and walks to me as soon as I step into the doorframe. "I want you to officially meet Andre."

"It is a pleasure to meet you," Andre says, taking my hand and bowing over it to place a formal kiss on the back. He just chuckles when Jager growls at him. "I've heard a lot about you. I'm glad to hear that your prowler was thwarted all those weeks ago."

"My... pro–? Oh gosh, the night it stormed?" I ask Jager and receive a nod in response.

"My meeting was with Andre that night," he tells me, pulling me into his side. "He almost came to the house with me."

"Funny enough, we were talking about how to legally take the club over for you. Guess that isn't so complicated anymore."

"For me?"

I really ask repeat questions too much. I need to work on that.

"You're the headliner, Poppy. I could take over the club on my own, but Andre has been looking to turn legit for a while now. I broached the subject of working together here."

"What about Mina?" I ask, eyes narrowed in warning.

"Mina's shares will double," Jager assures me, leaning down to kiss me as if I'm adorable for even asking. "You know I take care of my people."

Ugh, fine. That's definitely true. "So why were you working with Felix, then, huh?" I ask, summoning as much sass as possible but only eliciting a smile from Andre in return.

"Because he contacted me this evening and asked for help in 'dealing' with Conri. No one knows we're friends, and we like to keep it that way just for situations such as these. I would have called to warn him but you were here tonight before I had the time to step away from Felix."

"Oh."

"I promise. I may be up to a lot of illegal things, but I have never wanted to purchase a human. My interest in you and this club is merely your talent, and how I can use it to get out of the illegal dealings I have. It's getting as old as I am. Plus, my wife would kill me."

"Good to know," I smirk, finally relaxing and trusting that everything is ok. "So, what are we going to do with Trevor?"

"What do you want to do?" Jager asks, surprising me that he hasn't made that decision on his own.

"I…" I pause, thinking about what I truly want to happen to him. "I want him to share every hurt he put Gran and Mina through. And more."

"More?" Andre asks, seemingly impressed with my answer.

I can't help but smirk, a devious plan taking shape in my mind. No one harms the people I love and gets away with it. He hurt the people I love, which resulted in me killing a man. That can't be undone, so I'm going to lean into it.

"Oh, yes. Much more."

Chapter Twenty-One

I'm feeling nostalgic, so I decided tonight is the night to revisit my audition - with a few changes to show how much I've grown since then, of course. Jager wasn't too thrilled about it when I first told him what I wanted to do, but when I explained why I wanted it and what it really meant to me? He finally agreed. Grudgingly.

He was more than happy to alow Mike to inflict each injury Mina and Gran had received upon Trevor while I got ready, don't get me wrong, but the idea that his reserved table would not be his for my next performance? To say it did not sit well with him was an understatement. Only the promise of the second and third acts, plans of which I had to give him in great detail, could turn his pout into acquiescence.

I created a playlist and wrote up detailed lighting notes for Mike to provide to the DJ, requesting that he program it into the system before I take the stage. Everyone is welcome to stay for the first song, but the rest are only for the three of us.

Technically the two of us, once we count Trevor out.

I'm tying the final bow in my pigtails when Mike comes in carrying Mina. I jump up and rush to them, my cape falling off my shoulders since I hadn't secured it yet.

"Mina! Shouldn't you be resting? How are you feeling?"

"I'm fine!" she grumbles, then wiggles her eyebrows as she squirms around in his arms. "Mikey here won't let me walk but I refused the wheelchair, so until his arms are tired he's going to have be my personal stallion. He'll get tired of it eventually."

"We'll see about that," he mutters under his breath. "See if I ever let you out of my sight again."

She just laughs and kisses his cheek since it's the closest part of him to her. "Sugar, everything is all set to go. Patrons were kicked out and the staff who want to watch are all in the club proper."

"They know they have to leave at the end of the first song, right?"

"Right. We'll make sure of it. Oh! And here," she extends my phone, frowning as I look relieved to have it back.

"Thanks!" I breathe, happy someone found it. "Did I leave it in Jager's office earlier?"

"Mike found that on Felix."

"What? When?"

"When he was cleaning up the office. You didn't know he had it? We don't remember him taking it from you, but we were pretty distracted."

"No, I... I didn't have it at dinner, but I thought I accidentally left it in Jager's office or something." I unlock it and start looking through my messages. Gran never called like Trevor said, but I do see a text message I supposedly sent to her.

What the hell? Is Felix a pre-teen boy? Who texts like this?

"Oh my God, he texted my Gran with my phone! That's how they got her here."

"How'd he get it?" Mike asks, frowning. "Jager always keeps the door to the office locked."

"No idea. The only thing I can think of is when I used the restroom in the changing area before we left? I went in there because I wanted my favorite lipstick. I left my handbag on my vanity while I popped into the restroom, but I didn't see him at all while we were here."

"Sneaky fuck," Mike grumbles. "If you want I can have the phone looked over to make sure they didn't do anything to it."

"That would be amazing," I sigh, feeling lucky to have two friends like them. "Thank you."

"Any time," Mina answers for him, giggling as she accepts the phone back. "Are you ready?"

"Just about. I just need to freshen my lipstick. How's Gran doing? Do I have time to check on her?"

"Um, about that..." Mike hedges.

"What? What's wrong? Does she need to go to the hospital?"

I start rushing to my locker where my dress is hung, but I'm stopped and calmed immediately by Mina's forceful, "No! No, honey, she's totally fine."

"Then what's wrong?"

"She um... she wants to watch you dance." Mike's cheeks pink up adorably, as if he's embarrassed for me. In most circumstances something like that may be embarrassing, but not for us. Gran is my best friend, and I know she's proud of me. She used to dance too, so she isn't here to watch me shake my ass, she's here to watch me perform. Just like she was always there for my ballet recitals.

"Oh," I breathe, signing in relief and returning to my vanity to finish getting ready. "That's all? It's fine! She's watched me dance before over FaceTime when I was learning. She won't see anything that will scar her," I tell them, considering further. "Or me. Just make sure she leaves!"

"We've got you, Sugar."

"Thanks, guys. I mean it, I owe you both so much. I wouldn't have made it through the last few months without you."

"Consider it paid in full," Mike answers for them. "You have no idea what that man was like before he met you. Sometimes he even smiles now."

"I noticed that!" I laugh, proud that I can effect such change in a man like him. "Ok, let's go."

I take my place at the curtained edge of the stage with my hood over my face just as I did during my audition, but this time instead of Nine Inch Nails or my expected track for tonight I'm greeted with the voice of tonight's DJ, Walter.

"Allllllright everyone! We've got a special performance for you tonight coming from everyone's favorite redhead! Patrons know her as Ruby, spineless fuckwits don't know how to stop calling her Penny, and we all call her talented! But from now on alllllll you need to know is that she's the new boss!" I jerk, sticking my head out of the curtain and looking first to Jager, then Mina. She owned part of the club already, and Jager and Andre said she'd be getting larger shares. How can I be the boss?

Mina, sweet as ever, just grins and gives me two thumbs up while mouthing, "Trust me. It's ok." Gran is sitting next to her with wide, pride filled eyes.

That, more than anything in the world, makes everything we've just gone through worth it. I'm brought back to attention when Walter continues speaking. "That's right, but I'm not done yet! We've traded in two losers for not one but two lovely ladies! Mina, Ruby, take a bow!"

Relieved but still shocked, I step out and wave at everyone awkwardly while they all cheer, hug Mina, and surprisingly, send me happy waves and thumbs up.

I catch the eye of Walter and roll my hand in a "get on with it," gesture, and he straightens and nods before turning the lights down.

"Ok you rabble, settle down! You're getting a show, but after this song you know the rule–"

"We leave!" several of the waitresses yell together, laughing when he grumbles about being interrupted. I just shake my head and take my place by the pole, readjusting my cape and looking past the guest of honor to the only guest I actually care about. Knowing that I can have this business to fall back on while Gran is sick, and even if I still decide to go back to nursing school? I don't think Jager truly realizes the weight the gift he's just given me.

"Thank you," I mouth to him while the DJ reminds everyone to make sure they say goodbye to Trevor since they, "may not see him again."

I snort. You think?

They finally all settle and the lights hit their lowest as "Can You Feel My Heart" by Bring Me The Horizon begins. This time, unlike my audition, when I remove my cloak the dress hidden underneath is white instead of black and it glows vibrantly under the black lights pointed at me. I usually start my routines with heavy pole work, but I need my special guest to see and understand what's really happening here, so I make my way down the stage and drop to my knees in front of him.

Trevor looks awful. His face is swollen and his skin and hair are caked with blood. His fingers, ribs, and legs are broken, and he's tied to the same chair the guy used when I gave my first lap dance so I could take advantage of that swivel again. He watches as I continue to dance in front of him, and the only reason I'm still even looking at him is because I need to make sure he understands what I have for him next. I untie the sash to the white wrap dress and throw it open, smiling and winking at the DJ when he hits the cue perfectly. The crowd cheers when the lights change from black light to gels the second my crimson lingerie is revealed beneath the dress and it proves I made my point.

Bright red lingerie that covers only enough to keep him from seeing what I truly have to offer.

Because he'll never have it.

A vibrant, whorish red that proves exactly the kind of woman that I am.

One that no longer gives a single fuck about what he, or anyone else, thinks.

I release all of my bitterness, anger, and disdain for him in that moment and allow him to experience it in my gaze, then dismiss him the moment his first tear falls. I don't care if he's hurting! I'm hurting! He hurt the one person who has been there for me my entire life. After everything she and I have been through, he could have taken her from me for his own selfish reasons. There are no excuses or redemptions for that.

Once back at the pole I throw everything into my routine. I spin, climb, and slide until my breathing is so labored I feel as if I've run miles, but it's a complete catharsis. Every once in a while I hear his screams, his desperate pleas for help, but that only enhances my enjoyment. He didn't care about Gran and Mina's screams. Why would I care about his?

When "Gangsta" by New Years Day comes on I slow my dancing and soak up the cheers I that fade to the back of the club.

Time for phase two.

Descending the stairs at the edge of the stage I make my way to Trevor's chair to start his lap dance. Normally I wouldn't want to dance for him, but he's so securely tied to this chair and his fingers are so damaged I don't have to worry about him touching me without my permission. I also want him to suffer as much as possible before he dies, and I truly believe this will be the perfect mental and emotional torture. He was so desperate to be seated here when I auditioned, fighting with Jager and thinking his largesse in giving me a job would lead to me falling for him. He should have given up back then; his desperation is so much more palpable than it was before, but like that first night nothing he can say or do now will get him what he wants.

He can't have me, and he can't keep his life.

I immediately straddle him but completely ignore his existence and focus completely on Jager. It's like my first lap dance all over again, but so, so much better because I can fully admit exactly what I want. I shiver, half in disgust and half in arousal as I brush my breasts against Trevor, touching myself while watching the man across the room pull his dick out of his pants. They moved the table that usually sat in front of him at my request, so as I dance I'm able to watch every move he makes. My moves become more desperate until I find myself practically grinding on the nameless man beneath me while watching Jager stroke his cock.

Trevor is no longer a person. He's not some human with thoughts or feelings to be considered. He's a prop to be used for the gratification of the man in front of me, and when Trevor begins stiffening below me I tense and quickly stand. It's not from seeing Jager's dick because he's not facing him, so after I look behind me and confirm there's no one there I realize it must be because he's about to come in his pants. Sadly, it's not surprising after he came so quickly from masterbating in his office, but I refuse to allow the man a final release, especially at my expense. Straightening, I spin the chair so he's facing Jager and smile, knowing I'll be with him in a moment. Eventually I lean down and speak just loud enough in Trevor's ear that he has to strain to hear me over the music.

"I know you've always wanted me, Trevy-Poo," I tell him. "Even when we were in school together. But do you see him? The man sitting there in front of us looking like a fucking god with a monster cock? The man who can kill without a second thought?"

I wait for him to react, pausing until he finally nods jerkily.

"That is the man I love. He's not some boy who has to masterbate in his office while watching secret videos of women who will never want him." He stiffens at that and flinches away from me, trying to hide his face, so I grab his hair and make him look at me. Ignoring the cry of pain, I let him have it, scoffing at his complete incompetence.

"Oh, you didn't realize Jager had been licking my pussy on your desk while your door was locked? That he finger fucked me in your closet while you watched videos of me? While you played with your small dick and came in record time?" I tighten my grip for a moment then shove his head as far as his restraints will allow, disdain evident in every fiber of my being. I leave him with one parting shot before I make my way to Jager.

"How could I ever want you? You can call me a whore for not wanting you all you want, but you never gave me a good enough reason to. You never even respected me enough to call me by my fucking name."

Then I walk away.

I move toward my future and refuse to ever look at him again.

Chapter Twenty-Two

When I'm only steps away from Jager, Sleep Token's "Take Me Back To Eden" begins and I drop to my knees as if my strings have been cut. I tilt my head so my curls cover my face but allows the reflection of my eyes to shine through as I crawl to him, my exaggerated movements more languid than normal. My fingers reach the tips of his shoes and I sit up on my heels as I slide my fingers up the inseam of his pants, spreading his legs further apart so I can wedge myself in between them.

One hand still on is cock, Jager reaches up and brushes the hair out of my face and tilts my chin up so he can look at me unobscured.

"Such big, beautiful eyes you have, my sweet Poppy."

"Thank you," I breathe, blinking up at him and staring in awe as he lounges so confidently above me. "Better to see you with."

"Is that so? Hmm." he releases himself and lifts one of the hands I'm using to massage his thighs while we talk. "Such soft, strong fingers you have."

I hum, reveling in the sensation of his lips against the palm of the hand he's holding. I stop massaging his other thigh to wrap my fingers around his length and begin stroking him, knowing we're on the same page. "Better to touch you with," I tell him, my voice huskier than I thought possible. He releases my hand and slips his thumb into my mouth, growling as I begin to lick and suck on it without being asked.

"What a perfect fucking mouth you have."

I pull back, allowing his thumb to pop out from between my lips, then smile as I drop to lick him from base to tip.

"The better to taste you with."

I angle him toward my mouth and take him as deep as possible. I still need practice but I love the power I get from making him feel as good as he does me.

And honestly? I think he loves the fact that I'm inexperienced. Not only because he's been very clear he wants everything from me and that means he's gotten it, but because it means that as I discover my own sexuality, he can teach me, too.

I look up at him and quirk a brow in challenge, asking him without words why he isn't taking control of this situation. We both know he wants to, so he simply smiles and grips my hair, pressing me slowly down until my gag reflex begins to trigger. Instead of releasing me as he has in the past though, he holds me there for long enough that I have no choice but to relax or choke, so I relax.

"Good girl," he praises, "I knew you could do it. Soon, you'll be able to take all of me. Would you like that?" Unable to answer beyond a "mmph," I nod as much as his hold will allow. "Are you ready for me?" he asks, loosening his grip and pulling me off him.

I don't need to answer because I'm always ready for him.

I stand and reach behind me to untie my top so it can fall to the floor, then I straddle him with my legs to the outside of his in the large chair he chose. As much as I want to take him immediately inside of me I want to try a little something even more. We're in the club proper, and this is where lap dances are supposed to happen. I pull the strings tying my panties together and pull them both away, tossing the scrap of fabric to the side where I can find it again later. Smile, then take him in my hand once more and grind down on it to the beat of the pumping bass. I'm so wet he slides easily between my lips and I lean forward just enough to lick a path up the skin of his neck while each roll of my hips ensures I can rub his tip over my clit.

"My, my, Mr. Conri," I purr into his ear. "What a big, fat cock you have."

This time he doesn't hesitate when he grabs my hair. He snatches it without warning and uses that grip and his other hand on my ass to bend me almost backward until I'm straining to stay upright. The sting in my scalp and muscles is uncomfortable, but when he takes his dick from me and angles it to my opening I don't care - I'm getting exactly what I want.

"The better to fuck you with," he snarls, then forces me down so quickly I can't help but scream. The pleasure/pain line is completely blurred at this point. I can't decide if I'm hurting or about to come, but I think even if pain becomes the dominant sensation I'll still orgasm from it. He just plays my body that well.

I follow his lead, and the stretch and sensation that's created the further I lean back pushes me into the pleasure dominant spectrum. My eyes flutter shut as I allow him to support me with one hand at the back of my neck to help hold me up although I should be fine since I'm still kneeling on the chair.

I hope.

Pressure on my clit causes me to pop my eyes wide again and I remember we have an audience. Trevor was never supposed to experience things going this far, but I honestly forgot about him the moment I kneeled in front of Jager. He's staring at us with desperation and despair, and I just don't want to think about him anymore.

He doesn't get to share this moment with us.

Activating my core I do a situp while simultaneously tightening my muscles around him, pulling a groan from him. I lean over to the right where the table had been set and take up Jager's gun, handing it to him without missing a beat.

Part of me wants to kill him myself, but the larger part doesn't want to give him another second of my attention. Jager takes the gun as the screams of desperation intensify behind me, but other than checking the safety nothing changes in his movements - he never stops fucking me. His attention is solely focused on me as his arm extends toward Trevor, his eyes flick behind me for a fraction of a second, and then he kisses me as the shot rings out in the space.

I'm going to assume he's an amazing shot because the cries behind me stop immediately, but at this point I don't care anymore.

Let him watch, or let him die. Neither matters anymore..

All that matters to me is being in this moment with this man.

Trevor is forgotten by both of us as soon as the gun clatters to the floor and we simply lose ourselves in each other. My orgasm begins to build now that the stress of his impending demise has lifted and it feels to me as if it's building for him too. Our previously sensual and languid movements turn frantic, as if we cannot get enough skin to skin contact to satisfy our needs. In the frenzy of touch he unknowingly grabs the bruise I showed him earlier and that diversion back toward the pain line gave me exactly what I needed to climax. My body tightens and my pussy squeezes Jager so hard that he loses his own battle and joins me in bliss. The only thing holding me upright is him, and as soon as I'm able to move at all I can only fall forward and curl into his arms as I struggle to catch my breath.

He softens inside me, but neither of us want to move so I stay in place, snuggling into him once I calm and my body begins to shiver. Sometime later, how long I have no idea, fingers run through my hair and a quiet voice wakes me.

"Poppy," he calls, nuzzling the hair at my temple. "Sweetness, you need to wake up."

"Mmm?' I question, unaware that I had fallen asleep.

"Mike needs to bring the crew in here to clean up, and Mina needs to speak with you and your Gran."

"'Bout what?" I ask, yawning and unconcerned about anything but his warmth. I finally wake up, though, when I move and realize his dick is still inside me and beginning to stir again. My eyes widen in surprise and I look down, then back up to him. "Really?"

"Really. But, later. I know."

He helps me stand and tucks himself back into his pants as I scurry over to the stage to grab my trench coat and wrap up in it for warmth, all while purposely avoiding looking at the mess on the floor. Good thing it's dark tile, as owner I'd be the one to have to replace that carpet!

As soon as I'm covered he opens the far door and allows Mike and two other men entrance, each toting either a tarp or cleaning supplies.

"Mina and Ms. Channing are in your office, Pen," Mike tells me.

"But I don't have one yet," I argue, looking at Jager for confirmation.

"We figured you could take Trevor's," he tells me. "Mina likes being in the back with the girls so she can help them if they need it."

"Gross," I lament. "We need to rip that place down to studs. There's no telling how much desperate DNA has been sprayed all over the place."

I stopped in the changing room before going to my office so I could actually have some panties and real clothes on when speaking to my Gran, and I'm thankful for the warmth of the sweats that are kept here for anyone that needs them.

"Hi, Ladies," I call as I step into Trev– my office, Jager and Mike behind me. "What's up?'

"I don't know, Penny," Gran tells me, struggling to rise from her chair to come give me a hug. I rush to her side so she doesn't have as far to go and force her back into her seat so she can be as comfortable as possible. "She wouldn't tell me until you were here."

"Well, I'm just not sure what the situation is there, so I thought this would be the best option for everyone," Mina answers, worrying her lip as she struggles to sit in her own chair. "Someone called earlier and asked to set up a meeting with you."

"With me?" Gran asks, dumbfounded.

"No," Jager says, brow creased in concern. "With Penelope."

"Who? Who would want to talk to me?" No one knows I work here, so who could want to speak with me that makes Mina and Mike this nervous. "Is it the police or something?"

"No, Sugar," Mina says, standing again and stepping up next to me to take my hands, worrying me even more.

"It's your grandfather."

Also By JS Mercier

The Secrets Duet

The Rooms We Hide

The Secrets They Keep

Secrets: The Complete Duet
Secrets contains 2 exclusive short stories!

The Ghosts We Seek
Included in the What Lies In Darkness Anthology

The Void Prophecies

Exhale
Book 2 - Coming Soon
Book 3 - Coming Soon
Book 4 - Coming Soon

Radiant Poison
Originally Included in the Sacrilege Anthology

Cinnamon Roll Saviors

Safety

Short Story

The Jersey
Included in the Seeds of Love and Rebuilding Paradise
anthologies
Visit my website for a free copy!

www.ingramcontent.com/pod-product-compliance
Lightning Source LLC
Chambersburg PA
CBHW060421310726

48976CB00003B/1140

9 798991 232616